THE BABY MAKER

LILI VALENTE

SELF TAUGHT NINJA

THE BABY MAKER

By Lili Valente

The V-Card Diaries Series

Scored

Screwed

Seduced

Sparked

Scooped

Hot Royal Romance

The Playboy Prince

The Grumpy Prince

The Bossy Prince

Bad Motherpuckers Hockey

Hot as Puck

Sexy Motherpucker

Puck-Aholic

Puck me Baby

Pucked Up Love

Puck Buddies

Laugh-out-Loud Rocker Rom Coms

The Bangover

Bang Theory

Banging The Enemy

The Rock Star's Baby Bargain

Hometown Heat Series

All Fired Up

Catching Fire

Playing with Fire

A Little Less Conversation

The Bliss River Small Town Series

Falling for the Fling

Falling for the Ex

Falling for the Bad Boy

The Hunter Brothers

The Baby Maker

The Troublemaker

The Heartbreaker

The Panty Melter

Big O Dating Specialists
Romantic Comedies

Hot Revenge for Hire

Hot Knight for Hire

Hot Mess for Hire

Hot Ghosthunter for Hire

The Lonesome Point Series

(Sexy Cowboys)

Leather and Lace

Saddles and Sin

Diamonds and Dust

12 Dates of Christmas

Glitter and Grit

Sunny with a Chance of True Love

Chaps and Chance

Ropes and Revenge

8 Second Angel

The Good Love Series

(co-written with Lauren Blakely)

The V Card

Good with His Hands

Good to be Bad

The Happy Cat Series

(co-written with Pippa Grant)

Hosed

Hammered

Hitched

Humbugged

Some men are troublemakers or dealmakers. The men in my family? We're baby makers.

For six generations, the women of wine country have had a saying: don't bang a Hunter man unless you want a bun in your oven.

Yeah, well. I've got a saying, too: no thanks. The last thing I need is baby makes three. My business is expanding, and the only thing I'm interested in getting knocked up is my bottom line.

But then one night Emma Haverford makes me an offer I can't refuse—she backs away from the land I have my eye on in exchange for a favor...

A big, fat, baby-making favor...

* * *

When I hear women have gotten pregnant shaking hands with Hunter men, I know I need Dylan Hunter's...ahem, *special skills*...way more than I need to expand my vineyard.

I'm ready to give my heart to a child, and I'm tired of waiting for my late-to-the-party Prince Charming to make my dreams come true. So I promise Dylan: three months of hot, heavy, baby-making s-e-x, and then I'm out of his hair forever.

But what if when it comes time to say goodbye, all I want to do is keep bottling up more memories with this big-hearted man?

This sexy stand-alone romance will make you laugh, swoon, and blush baby-makin' red. Heat level: a risk of getting knocked up during download. Paperback and audio versions are especially dangerous. Handle with care...

Dedicated to Lauren Blakely
for excellence in the field of cover image hunting.
Thank you, mama!

CHAPTER 1

DYLAN

*H*ere's the thing about days that change your life…

When you wake up, you have no idea you're on the cusp of a life changer.

Your alarm goes off at five a.m. like any other day. You yawn, curse the cold floor waiting to bite your foot as soon as you swing a leg out from under the covers, and start the usual routine.

You chug a glass of water, trudge through the sleeping house to the back door, and run down the list: feed the dogs, water the chickens, move the mobile coops across the still damp grass, milk the cow your younger brother adopted before he moved just far enough away to make it impossible for him to milk Moo-Donna—a rescue cow with a bad attitude and unusually sharp teeth—and slam a fist on the guest house door to get your nephews out of bed because your older brother wants them doing chores while they're staying with you, even though it would be easier to gather the eggs yourself.

Getting teenagers out of bed is usually akin to hauling large boulders up a mountain against a gale force wind while birds peck out your eyeballs, and this morning is no different.

"Jacob! Blake!" I shout, pounding on the door again. "The eggs need to be sorted for the restaurant orders and the extras on the stand before seven."

Mumbles and groans seep through the thin door, followed by a plaintive, "Five more minutes. It's Saturday, Uncle Dylan."

"Which means people will be out walking the trail behind the house, looking for eggs to take home for breakfast," I counter. "Up. Now. Go."

I thump the door three more times for good measure and head back to the house, thinking grumbly thoughts about the list of chores I had as a seventeen-year-old and the way things were done back in *my* day.

I'm thirty-one, way too young for old-fart belly-aching, but that doesn't stop me from growling at Rafe as I duck into the kitchen, "I should make the boys milk the cow. Let them get chewed a few times and they'll be grateful for egg duty."

Rafe, who's tying on his work boots for the first time in longer than I can remember, laughs. "You sound like Dad."

"I don't sound like Dad." I scowl harder as I grab the truck keys off the hook. "You going to be around today?"

"Where else would I be? If I'm staying here, I'm

working here." Rafe arches a dark brow as he stands. My half-brother has his Italian mother's dark hair and olive skin, but people still mistook us for twins when we were kids.

But then, we are only two months apart in age. That kind of thing happens when your father has a habit of spreading the love around.

And around...

And around...

Before a prostate cancer fight finally slowed him down, Dad managed to have four sons by three different women. My mom was the one he *didn't* marry, the hippie he met at a music festival in Mendocino, knocked up, and saw a few times a year until she got tired of the single-mother gig, dropped me off at Dad's, and never came back.

I've been here ever since. This land has its claws in me deep, and most days I'm okay with that. Grouchy thoughts aside, I love what I do, especially this time of year, when the hops harvest is in and all I've got on my plate is managing the organic egg arm of our operation. Though, I am looking forward to the day when I get to keep the hops for myself, start my own brewery, and make a name for the Hunters with beer the way my great-granddad did with wine.

I'm so close to having our debts paid, my well-oiled growing machine in prime working order, and the reins ready to hand over to Dad.

Or, better yet, a manager I will pay to make sure Dad's stress levels stay low and my well-oiled machine doesn't break down. The farm was struggling when I took over three years ago, and I don't want any back-sliding.

"Thanks for taking my ass in," Rafe continues, crossing the faded brown tile. "I appreciate it."

I shake my head and scoff at his crazy. "Get out. Your house burned down, man. Like we're going to let you stay in a hotel for months while you wrestle with the insurance company. Besides, this is your home. You're always welcome."

"I know. But I also know you've got a lot on your plate," he says, gaze lifting pointedly toward the ceiling. "He still giving you shit?"

"Daily," I say dryly. "A fresh load every afternoon, like clockwork."

Rafe rolls his eyes. "Yeah, well, fuck that. You're killing it, Dylan. This ship was headed for the rocks, and you turned it around. Just let Dad's bitching go in one ear and out the other."

I grunt as we swing out of the back door and load into my truck for the drive into town. I know he's right, but my father's complaining still gets to me. Pop doesn't care that growing hops to sell to local breweries and producing sustainably farmed eggs is making us just as much money as growing grapes ever did. He doesn't care that diseased vines nearly cost us our land, the house, the farm, and everything our family has worked hundreds of years to build. He loves wine as much as he loves women, and I'm the bad guy who took the grapes away from him.

The only way to get him off my back and on board with the path I've chosen is to get him what he wants.

Vines.

Vines close enough he can glimpse them out his bedroom window before he goes to sleep at night, the way it used to be when our land was acres of pinot noir as far as the eye could see. And there's only one way I'm going to be able to deliver that. I need the three acres on the other side of the multi-use trail that runs along the back of our property.

I need that fucking pumpkin patch.

By rights, it should be mine. Farmer Stroker and I are tight. I've personally picked at least half the pumpkins on that land for years, for God's sake. There should be no "considering other offers."

And there wouldn't be if *she* hadn't shown up.

My shoulders tense and my grip tightens on the steering wheel as thoughts of *her* further the grouchification of my morning. It's almost enough to make me turn right at the first stop sign in town. Almost enough to make me choose bitter drive-in coffee instead of Barn Roasters' Sonoma County brew.

Almost, but not quite.

Even the risk of running into She Who Will Not Be Named can't convince me to knock back third-rate coffee-flavored swill. I appreciate coffee the way Pop appreciates wine, and I will not subject my mouth to a caffeinated atrocity when there is hot, steamy, black gold waiting at the end of Main Street.

Besides, last night I promised Rafe one of Sophie's cinnamon rolls as a "sorry your house and shop burned down" present, and I'm a man who keeps his promises.

At the end of Main, I roll into the rocky parking lot

in front of Barn Roasters, which is already filled with mud-splattered pickups, a smattering of shiny rental cars from the wine-tasting tourists who have done their homework, and a gaggle of bicycles leaning against the faded gray planks of the old barn turned coffee house, testimony to the shop's location just off the scenic bike trail that winds through Mercyville and into the city of Santa Rosa.

Of course, at least half of those city-dwelling cyclists are going to be pissed that they can't check their email while they're slugging back a local brew.

Cell reception is shitty in town, and Barn Roasters is rustic all the way—no wifi, no tables, no bells and whistles, just a bar twenty-five feet long where people can pull up a stool and enjoy an extraordinary cup of joe and the view across the hills through the windows.

It's one of my favorite places on earth. Has been for years. A cup of Sophie's coffee is my favorite way to start the day, and I'm not going to change that, not even to avoid another unpleasant interaction with the Blonde Terror.

"Think of the devil," I mutter as Rafe and I open the door, releasing a puff of cinnamon, sugar, and dark-roast scented air and granting me a perfect view of a perky ponytail sidled up to the bar on my left.

Emma Haverford, thorn in my side, salt in my wound, paper cut in my eye, has beaten me to coffee yet again.

She's wearing overalls today—faded blue-jean overalls with mud stains on the cuffs over a tight red T-shirt —with a crisp red bandana tied in her hair.

"Playing farmer dress-up again, are we?" I ask as I pass behind her on the way to two empty stools at the far end of the bar.

She turns, smiling pleasantly, her big blue eyes wide behind her wire-rimmed glasses.

Damn it, why couldn't she have taken two minutes to slip in contacts? I *hate* those glasses. They make her look like a sexy librarian you secretly want to shush you for talking too loud...

"Still supercilious this morning, I see," she coos in response, lifting her espresso in a one-sided toast.

I scrunch my brow into an exaggerated scowl. "Ease up with the big words, little lady. We're simple folks around here. We don't traffic in more than three syllables."

"Yeah, right," she says, still grinning. "You don't fool me Dylan Hunter. You're smarter than you look. I bet you know at least two synonyms for patronizing."

My scowl falls away as my under-caffeinated synapses struggle to whip up a snappy comeback. After a few seconds—never leave smartassery unaddressed for more than five, six tops—I shrug and shoot her my "oh-hell, honey" grin, the one that's been getting me out of trouble and successfully rounding third base since I was sixteen. "All right. Your point this time, Blondie. You're lucky I haven't had coffee yet."

She tips her head smugly, clearly enjoying her victory. "Take your time. I'll be here tomorrow. Not going anywhere."

The seemingly innocent words set my teeth on edge again. Because I hear them for what they are—a threat, a promise that she's not going to sell out like most of the Silicon Valley refugees, people who come seeking romance and adventure in wine country only to go running back to their cushy tech jobs when they realize how much hard work and risk-taking is involved in farming for a living.

Because growing grapes to make wine is, at its heart, farmer's work. Not billionaire's work. Not movie star's work. Not something glamorous you do in your spare time in between sipping chardonnay on your patio. Running a successful vineyard takes stamina and grit combined with intimate knowledge of the land.

There's no doubt in my mind that Blondie is missing at least two of the three. She's clearly stubborn as hell, but junior college agriculture classes are only going to take her so far. Sooner or later, she's going to run into a wall too high for her petite self to climb, and I'll be there, ready to make the most of her moment of weakness.

"Damn," Rafe murmurs as we settle onto our stools and I signal Sophie for two coffees. "That the new neighbor? The one who bought the Parker place?"

"Yep." I fold my arms on top of the bar, keeping my gaze out the window where the morning sun paints the vineyards hazy shades of pink and gold, determined not to give Ms. Haverford another second of my attention. "That's the one."

"She doesn't look like Satan's little sister," Rafe observes, clearly amused. "In fact, she's pretty damned cute. Petite, but curvy, and those eyes..." He hums

8

appreciatively. "I've never seen eyes that big and blue in real life. Almost like a cartoon, but sexy. Is that crazy?"

I shake my head, determined to shut this down before it goes any further. "Yes. It's crazy. Don't even start with her. She's the enemy. Stroker had all but signed over the deed to that property. Then she swooped in, offered ten grand over the asking price, and now suddenly he's got to think things over."

Rafe shrugs. "Ten grand is a lot of money."

"I've been helping him bring in his harvest every October since I was twelve years old. I'm like a grandson to him—his words—and that's not how you're supposed to treat family." I let out a long breath and drop my volume, making sure my next words are for Rafe's ears only. "And she doesn't date, anyway. Word through the grapevine is she's turned down every guy who's asked her out. Prefers staying home alone with a book."

A book she probably looks really hot reading in those sexy glasses...

"That may be so," Rafe says, a wicked grin curving his lips. "But she hasn't had a Hunter man ask her out, has she?" His smile widens. "Or is that really why you can't stand her, bro? Did you ask and she said no?"

I make a just-drank-lemon-juice-straight face that I hope expresses how much offense I take to his sugges-tion. "Hell, no. All I want from that woman is for her to stop interfering with this deal, stop complaining when I rip out blackberry bushes along the shared property line, stop riding her bicycle through town and slowing down traffic, and quit taking up a stool at *my* coffee shop and ruining my favorite half hour of the day."

"Two coffees, extra cream and just a little sugar," Sophie says, setting down two heavy white mugs on the scarred bar. "What else can I get you? Biscuit? Cinnamon roll? I've also got oatmeal with almonds and honey this morning."

Rafe orders a cinnamon roll, and I opt for the oatmeal. Sophie shouts the order to the two younger women working the kitchen and then turns back to Rafe with a warm smile. "What're you doing in town so early, doll? When was the last time you were in for morning coffee? A year ago, maybe two?"

From there, the conversation turns to the fire that consumed Rafe's shop/apartment in downtown Santa Rosa, as well as a trendy restaurant, a tattoo parlor, and several other shops. Sophie—who has always had a soft spot for Rafe—clucks and fusses over him, repeating what everyone in our family's said at least a dozen times since we got the call from him yesterday letting us know he was safe.

"Well, at least you're okay. You're the only thing that can't be replaced." She lays a freckled hand on his forearm and gives it a squeeze. "And it's good to have you back in town. Don't be a stranger, okay?"

"I won't," Rafe promises, nodding my way. "This one has to have the good stuff every morning, so I expect I'm going to be a regular."

Sophie nods seriously, setting the red-and-gray bun atop her head bobbing. "Good. Life's too short to drink shitty coffee. Dylan gets it. Learn from him. He's a smart kid."

Rafe laughs. "Smarter than he looks, anyway."

I narrow my eyes, but that only makes the bastard laugh harder. He's in excellent spirits for a man who just lost half a million dollars in vintage Harleys and parts. But they were insured, and Rafe has never been the kind to sweat the small stuff.

Or the big stuff. He doesn't sweat much, in fact. He just jumps on his chopper and heads for the hills when things get hairy.

If anyone's going to be learning lessons around here, it should be me. Rafe would never have let himself get so tangled up in a web of obligation that it's going to require surgical extraction to get my life back on a track of my own choosing.

But I'll manage. This is my year.

Mine. And no one, certainly not a perky blonde from the city who has no idea what it's like to work her ass off to cultivate every acre under her care, is going to get in my way.

I shift my glare in Emma's direction, but she's already gone.

Which is good. I've been doing my best to keep the ribbing between us light. I don't want her to realize how much she truly gets to me, or how many hours I lie awake at night trying to figure out how to convince Stroker to choose me without my having to go deeper into debt. I could get an extra ten or fifteen grand, but it would cost me more precious months of freedom to earn it back.

And I'm afraid if I don't start making my aspirations reality soon, I never will. And then that brewery with my name on it will be just another dream I put aside to do what was best for the Hunter clan.

I love my family and our farm, but it's time my life belonged to me.

By the time Rafe and I have finished turning the hops in the drying kiln late in the afternoon—passing back and forth from the kiln to the barn at least a dozen times, taking in the view of the orange-speckled pumpkin patch below—my mind is made up. I'll talk to Stroker tomorrow and convince him we should put our heads together until we come up with an acceptable counteroffer that doesn't include more cash up front. I can promise him the twins as harvest slaves for this year —my older brother, Deacon, is deployed with his unit until spring, so the boys are at my mercy until then— and maybe let Stroker stay on at his farmhouse after the sale. The man is eighty-five years old and probably not thrilled about moving at his age.

Yes. This is going to work. I can feel it. Optimism fizzes in my bloodstream, promising that things are starting to look up.

And then it happens.

That life-changing thing.

It wrenches me out of bed in the dead of night and sets me on a collision course with destiny.

Destiny that comes in an unexpected perky blond package...

CHAPTER 2

EMMA

*C*ritical mass: (physics) the amount of a fissionable material necessary to sustain a chain reaction at a constant rate.

—Nuclear Chemistry Flash Cards Emma Haverford Never Threw Away After Undergrad

MOST PEOPLE ARE familiar with critical mass. If not the physics concept, then in the figurative sense. Critical mass is when someone reaches the end of her rope, when the straw breaks the camel's back, when she simply can't take it anymore.

Critical mass is when shit gets real.

For me it started at around seven a.m. Saturday morning, when Dylan Hunter swaggered into my favorite coffee shop wearing a pair of faded jeans that hugged his muscled thighs, leaving nothing about his drool-worthy body to the imagination. The man is built like a Greek god or a superhero or one of those guys who enter lumberjack competitions for a living. He's preposterously good looking, a head-turner no matter what your sexual preference.

Gay, straight, bi, not-all-that-interested-in-nookie-at-this-life-juncture-thank-you—it doesn't matter. When a man with that kind of raw animal magnetism passes by, you can't help yourself.

You turn, you look, maybe you drool a little if you didn't sleep well the night before and are having trouble controlling your body's involuntary responses.

And even though the way he teases me like the new girl in school who swooped in to steal his Star Student award drives me up the wall, his sleepy hazel eyes and crooked smile work their dark magic the way they always do. Even as my lips are saying all the right things —sassy, confident things that prove I'm not about to let this man bully me into backing away from something I want—I know my eyes are saying something entirely different.

My eyes are making invitations that haven't been cleared by my brain or my heart, while tingling sensations race across my skin and something deep in my core yearns toward Dylan like a moth to a flame.

But we all know what happens to the moth when it finally scores a hug from fire, right?

It burns. It suffers. And then it dies. Bye-bye moth, better luck next incarnation. Hopefully you'll be born with a better sense of self-preservation.

Luckily, I am not a moth.

I am a woman who knows better than to mess with men like Dylan.

I snuff out the yearning with another shot of espresso, get my oatmeal to go, and ignore the way the morning sun glints off Dylan's sandy blond hair as he laughs at something the man next to him—his brother, I think, though we haven't been introduced—is saying.

I moved to Sonoma County to embrace the beauty of life—*real* life, not the virtual existence I'd been sleep-walking through for years—but some beautiful things are best observed from afar. No matter how lonely my evenings have been, the last thing I need is a fling with a commitment-phobe who thinks I'm Satan's hand-maiden and hasn't been in a long-term relationship since his senior year of high school.

Bless small town gossip for keeping me in the know.

I'm sure it will come back to bite me on the butt sooner or later, but so far, I appreciate getting the scoop on my new neighbors. It's like a map marking the safe path through a minefield of interpersonal relationships going back generations. As the new girl in a small, small town, I need all the help I can get.

On my way out of Barn Roasters, I pause to hold the door for a young mother with a stroller, and the baby—an angel-faced little boy with oodles of dark curls—flashes me a gummy smile.

The yearning I thought I'd smothered with espresso blazes to life again, even fiercer than before.

It's different than the pull toward a beautiful man, but it springs from the same source—from the need to connect, to create, to love and be loved. It springs from the river of emotion damned up deep inside of me, desperate to be set free to flow out into the world.

Less than a year ago, I was positive a baby was in my future. My *near* future. I had an engagement ring on my finger and a chart on my bedside table tracking the days when I was most likely to conceive. Jeremy and I joked about being rebels, bucking tradition and going for baby-makes-three before we walked down the aisle.

Later, he would tell me that I was already married to my job. That the seventy hours a week I spent writing code for a top Internet search engine was the reason he didn't want to set a wedding date, the reason he wanted to get me pregnant, so I would be forced to slow down, the reason he eventually had an affair and left me for another woman.

Now, I don't know if I'll ever have a husband or children.

Though, at this point in my life, it's the loss of those dream babies that cuts a hole in my chest the size of the prize-winning pumpkins in Farmer Stroker's patch. I ache for them in a way I've never ached for anything, proving you can be haunted by something you've never had.

The thought follows me back to my house on the edge of my new property's ten-acre vineyard, making the silence I usually appreciate feel like a portent. I will always be alone, in silence. There will never be a voice calling out to welcome me home, or a child's laughter in the garden, or any of the family sounds I remember from my early years, that golden time before my parents' split and my sister Carrie and I became painful reminders of what they had lost.

I shower, change into clean clothes, and grab my backpack full of worksheets and today's lesson plan, determined to buck up and enjoy the rest of the day. But despite the early autumn sun warming my skin and the smell of squishy blackberries fermenting on the vine perfuming the air as I ride my bike to the elementary school, my worldview remains gloomy.

My two-hour weekend class, Cool Girls Code, allows me to put my old life to use enriching my new one, helping the next generation of girls confidently take their place in the computer science field. So far, I've been working with ten girls, ages five through fifteen, and they are all lovely, intelligent, sweet, and curious ladies who make me feel hopeful about the future.

But today their smiles and laughter, their victory cries and groans of frustration as a line of code that worked in the command window fails to run inside the function, don't warm me in the usual way.

Instead, they are fingers probing a bruise, reminding me where it hurts.

It hurts right *there*, in the center of my stupidly lonely heart. And when seven-year-old Isabella gives me a hug on her way out the door—telling me that she's going to bring me some of her *abuela's* homemade tortillas next week for our lunch break—it's all I can do not to break down and cry.

Yes, I nearly start weeping in front of my shiny, happy students. So I do what any self-respecting woman would do—I grab a bar of gourmet dark chocolate from the farmer's market on the way across town and eat the entire thing. Screw keeping my caffeine and sugar consumption under control.

Desperate times call for chocolate-intense measures.

I arrive at my two o'clock doctor's appointment with my blood buzzing, which unfortunately does nothing to make my annual lady parts examination any less uncomfortable. Dr. Seal seems like a kind, compassionate woman, but I would swear she pulled that speculum out of the deep freeze seconds before I arrived.

The exam room is freezing, too, so even after the worst is over, I can't help feeling like a slab of meat prepped for the butcher.

"Relax...deep breaths," Dr. Seal says, gently prodding at my abdomen as I stare at the square tiles on the ceiling. "Any pain here?"

"A little." I clench my teeth to keep them from chattering. "But I've been hitting the caffeine pretty hard lately, so I'm sure that's part of it."

"Not great for endometriosis," she says mildly, repeating what I heard from my OB back in Palo Alto before I moved. "But I'm sure you know that."

I smile. "Yes, but I love coffee more than I hate pain."

She laughs, motioning for me to sit up. "Understandable. But if the cramping gets too bad, let's talk about what you might want to eliminate from your diet, okay?"

"Got it," I say, smoothing my gown down over my knees.

"So is there anything else you wanted to discuss today?" Dr. Seal asks, her brown eyes warm. "I'm assuming you have birth control in place that works for you?"

"Um, yes. I do." I clear my throat as I nod. Swearing off relationships until I've got everything at the winery and tasting room running smoothly is certainly effective birth control, but I know that's not what she means.

"Great. But if you decide you want to explore other options, give us a call. It can take time to get an appointment with me on busy weeks, but Nancy, our nurse practitioner, is wonderful and can always talk you through your options."

"Speaking of options," I find myself saying before I realize that I'm going there.

I didn't plan to discuss *this* today—I have enough on my plate without adding another major life change into the mix—but now that I've started I don't want to stop.

"I'm wondering about...babies," I say, pulse speeding simply from speaking the word aloud. "I'd like to have a child sooner rather than later, but my ex and I tried for nearly a year without any luck, and I know endometriosis can make conception more difficult. Do you think I should start trying soon? If I want to have a baby before thirty-six or thirty-seven?"

I have no idea how I'm going to start "trying" at this point, but if Dr. Seal says the time is ripe, I guess I can start checking out the local sperm banks.

The doctor's brow furrows as she rolls her chair

over to the computer screen, glancing at my chart. "You're thirty-four?"

"Yes," I confirm. "Thirty-five in a few months."

She hums low in her throat. "Assuming there's room in your life for a child now, I would encourage you and your partner to go ahead and start tracking your cycle and timing intercourse on your most fertile days. And if you don't conceive within six months this time, then we can discuss more aggressive options. I can walk you through those myself, or refer you to a colleague of mine who specializes in pregnancy in women of advanced maternal age."

I laugh, but her expression assures me she's not kidding. "Um, advanced maternal age? I...I'm not there already, am I? I mean, I thought I had time. At least a little."

"You absolutely have time," she says, in a voice I can tell is meant to be reassuring, but isn't. "But traditionally, women aged thirty-five or older are considered to be of advanced maternal age. Fertility decreases rapidly between the ages of thirty-one and thirty-seven, and then even more rapidly as you move toward forty. As long as you know you want a child, it makes sense to start as soon as possible. So I'll give you a prescription for prenatal vitamins, instructions on how to track fertility, and hopefully we'll be able to get you on the road to becoming a mom soon."

Becoming a mom...

Oh my God. A *mom*...

Tears spring into my eyes, but they aren't sad tears this time. They're hopeful tears. Honest tears. Tears that assure me that *yes*, this is what I want, what I long for more than anything, what I need to make my life complete. I need that little boy or little girl I've been dreaming of for so long in my arms, in my heart, where I will keep him or her forever.

Swallowing past the lump in my throat, I nod, smiling through the mistiness blurring the edges of Dr. Seal's face. "Yes, that sounds perfect."

And it does.

But it's also…complicated.

As I wander out the door and make my way toward where I parked my bike near the town square, I start asking the harder questions like—do I really want to have a stranger's baby? Some guy who spent a few minutes jerking off to porn in a windowless room in exchange for whatever sperm banks are paying for deposits these days? Sure, I'll be able to check out his genetic history, education, and I think they even show pictures sometimes, but I won't be able to look into the man's eyes in real time and see if he's one of the good guys.

I'm a big proponent of the gut check. I don't care how good you look on paper, if you trigger a "not safe" signal in my lizard brain, we're not going to be friends, let alone create a life together. I'm not sure if creepiness is an inheritable trait, but I'm not willing to risk it, at least, not as long as I have other options.

But do I? And if so, what are they?

A few minutes later, I guide my bike into the winery's drive and keep going, past the tasting room where Denver and Neil, my two ruthlessly charming hosts, are pouring wine for three couples who arrived in a stretch limousine.

Usually I would pop in to say hello and visit for a while, but I need to conserve my energy. Bart, my vineyard manager, told me this morning that the grape sugar levels are right where I want them to be. Which means we'll be starting our harvest at two a.m. tonight to ensure the fruit doesn't get warm on the way from the vine to the crush pad.

That also means an afternoon pleasure ride isn't in my future. But that doesn't mean I can't find a place to enjoy the sights.

I roll onto the multi-use trail that runs through the heart of the Green Valley wine region. It's truly a stunning gift to the people of this county, chock-full of rolling hills, vineyards, apple orchards, and adorable Wine Country cottages, with plenty of strategically placed benches for sitting and enjoying the breathtaking views.

Today, my favorite bench—the one dedicated "To Grandma Mona with All our Love," with a vista of my own vines—is taken by two women in their mid-twenties, sharing a bottle of wine, a basket full of goodies, and a serious case of the giggles.

The sight makes me lonesome for my sister, who also happens to give tremendous advice in times of trial.

Once I've parked my bike and settled on my second-favorite bench a few yards away from the other women, I pluck my phone from my basket and pull up Carrie's contact info. I'm trying to decide whether to text or call, when Giggler Number One says something so interesting, I can't help but pause to eavesdrop.

"Seriously. The Hunter men are famous for it. Women stand too close to them, and they end up pregnant. It doesn't even require penetration. A Hunter man can knock you up with a hug. Even a handshake is dangerous."

Her friend laughs. "Stop it. You're scaring me."

"You should be scared," Giggler One insists, doubling down. "This isn't an urban legend. This is the real thing, backed up by a family tree with more branches than spokes on my bicycle. Hell, you might be pregnant already just from the intense eye contact you and Rafe had going on."

Friend starts giggling again. "Oh my God, it *was* intense. He's so incredibly hot."

"So hot," Giggler One agrees.

"So I don't care if he's got super sperm." Friend swirls the straw-colored liquid in her glass with a jaunty wiggle of her shoulders. "My diaphragm and I are going in, girlfriend. It's been too long since I've been with someone who looks like that in jeans."

But Dylan looks even better, I silently add.

Dylan looks *phenomenal* in jeans, and he's also a Hunter, one of these hypermasculine creatures rumored to have legendary fertility. And he's not a creep, not even close. From everything I've heard around town, if you're not bidding against him for a piece of property, he's a nice guy. And even though I'm clearly not his favorite person, he's never been unkind to me.

He just…doesn't like me very much.

Right. He doesn't like *you, psycho, let alone* LIKE *you. Why on God's green earth, would he even consider putting a bun in your oven?*

"Because I have something he wants," I murmur aloud, text and call forgotten.

I tap the edge of my cell against my lips, heart racing as a plan begins to form.

CHAPTER 3

*I*t's a wild plan.

A crazy plan.

But a plan that might have a happy ending for everyone involved.

Yes, I want Mr. Stroker's land—it would be the perfect place to plant more cool weather Zinfandel, and it's right next to property I already own—but I want a baby more. And if I promise Dylan that no one ever has to know, that it will be our secret, just the two of us until the day I die, maybe…

Just maybe…

I tell myself crazier things have happened. I tell myself super sperm is worth risking rejection and a mortifying "hell, no," from a repulsed and outraged Dylan. I tell myself that I am a she-warrior and now isn't the time to shy away from battle. I left a cushy job in Silicon Valley to run a vineyard with only three community college Ag classes and several years of Custom Crush hobby winemaking under my belt. I sold everything I owned—house and rental property—and sank it all into this dream I'm making come true with long days of hard work and a killer five-year business plan.

But a dream come true doesn't amount to much without someone to share it with. Someone to pass it on to…

Back home, the three couples emerge from the tasting room as I'm biking up the path. The sight of the baby seat one of the women carries cuts through the last of my hesitation, searing away my doubt.

That baby carrier is *a sign*.

Everything that's happened today, from wanting to jump Dylan's bones at the coffee shop, to the baby in the buggy, to the little girl hugs and the doctor warning me it's time to get busy, to the perfectly-pertinent conversation I just happened to overhear—they are *all* signs. This is my destiny, a challenge from the universe to see if I intend to keep that promise I made as I drove north on the 101 with everything I own in the back of a moving van.

Am I really going to grab life with both hands and squeeze every bit of joy from it that I can get? Or am I going to be a coward who sits on the sidelines, waiting for someone else to decide if they can spare some happiness to toss my way?

"No," I say aloud, rolling my bike into the barn, where I've turned the old tack room into bike and kayak storage.

I'm not going to sit and wait.

I'm going to act!

Soon. Very soon.

* * *

BUT I HONESTLY DON'T EXPECT IT to be that very night. I don't expect the engine to blow on the rolling overhead lights Bart and I just checked out last week. I don't expect Bart to run over to the Hunter place to borrow their light cart to ensure the safety of our harvest workers.

I don't expect Dylan to tow the light over with his tractor, or stick around to fuss over the broken engine with Bart, agreeing that a bum alternator is to blame. And I certainly don't expect to be walking him back to his place after he graciously offers to leave his tractor so Bart can tow the light back to him in the morning.

But here I am, flashlight in hand, soft moonlight overhead, and Dylan so close I can smell the laundry detergent, dust, and healthy male scent of him. He smells good enough to eat, or at least to bite. All over. One sexy inch of flesh at a time.

Making a baby with him wouldn't be a hardship, that's for sure…

But how to start a conversation like this?

Where do I even begin?

"Thank you again," I say, my voice thin and trembly. I clear my throat, willing myself to woman up as I add, "I really appreciate the help. I can't believe that light went out. It's barely a year old, and Bart and I both ran checks on it last week."

Dylan shrugs. "It's no big deal. I know how it is.

Something always breaks at the worst possible time. It's the Murphy's Law of Harvest."

"Oh good," I say with a laugh. "I mean, not good, but at least it's not a sign that the wine gods are against me."

"No, I think the wine gods like you just fine. Your grapes look great this year." He hums contemplatively. "Though, the Pumpkin King might have something against you, now that I think about it."

I peer up at him in the dim light under the trees. "The Pumpkin King?"

"Yeah, the spirit who haunts the pumpkin patch." He jabs a thumb toward Mr. Stroker's property. "Doesn't like pretty blond women? Would prefer a man who knows his way around this land to lay claim to his three acres?"

I stop on the trail, which is abandoned at this time of night, nothing but a winding ribbon of silver and shadow in both directions as far as the eye can see. But the light is better here, giving me a clear view of Dylan's teasing expression. "So you're saying the Pumpkin King is a sexist jerk?"

He grins. "Nah, he just likes guys."

"So it's a sexual preference thing?"

Dylan winks. "Exactly."

My pulse spikes and panic oozes into my blood-stream, cold and shocking.

Oh my God, does Dylan...?

Could he... Could I have read him all wrong?

Unable to stop myself, I blurt out, "And what about you?"

"What about me?"

I clear my throat again, aiming for a casual tone. "Do you like guys?"

"Um, no, not in that way." He laughs softly, a low rumble that's warm and lovely.

"Oh. Good. Thank God." My breath rushes out as I press my hand to my chest. I'm so relieved that it takes me a second to realize how that must have sounded.

By the time I do, Dylan's studying me with a cocked head and arched brows.

"I mean, I d-don't have anything against gay people," I stammer, waving an awkward hand in the air between us. "I like gay people. Love them! I have lots of gay friends back in the city, and Neil, my tasting room host, is gay. I just meant..." I shake my head with a laugh. "I meant I'm, um..." I pat my throat, fighting my nerves as my brain screams to spit it out already and my pride demands that I abort this mission, run home, hide under my bed, and pretend this interaction never happened.

Dylan nods slowly. "You're what, Blondie?" His voice is deeper, huskier than it was a moment before.

My gaze lifts sharply, connecting with Dylan's. There's an almost audible sizzle, and my heart gallops faster. It's been a while for me, but that certainly *looks* like interest of a more-than-friendly variety flickering across his features.

Time to go for it. All in. No backing down now.

I lift my chin, maintaining eye contact as I utter the six terrifying words that have been floating around my head all night. "I have a favor to ask."

"What kind of favor?"

"A big favor," I continue breathlessly, enough adrenaline coursing through my veins to make me feel like I'm chugging uphill on a roller-coaster, headed for one hell of a drop. "But before you say no, I want to promise you that no one ever has to know about this. And when I make a promise, I keep it. Forever. I will take this secret to the grave if that's what you want. And I'll withdraw my bid on the Stroker property tomorrow so it will be yours, free and clear."

His brow furrows. "You're a confusing woman, Blondie."

"I'm sorry," I say, nibbling on my lip.

He shakes his head. "It's fine. I just thought I had an idea where you were going with that, and then you hit one into left field. So what is it you want me to do for you in exchange for withdrawing your bid?"

"I, uh..." I attempt a deeper breath, but my ribs are in stress-induced lockdown. No more air is getting in, so I had better use what I have left to get the words out. "I want a baby."

Dylan's brows shoot up so high and fast it would be funny if I weren't so desperate for him to agree to my plan.

"I know I could use a sperm donor," I barrel on, figuring if I'm in for a penny I might as well gamble it all. "But I don't want a stranger's baby. I want someone I know is a nice guy, and everything I've heard about you has been great. People around here love you and respect you. And I know you don't like me, but we wouldn't have to be friends. It could just be something we do for a few months to see if it works, and if it doesn't, then

30

that's fine." I wave what I hope is a breezy hand. "No harm, no foul, and you still have what you want. Even if I don't get pregnant."

He makes a strangled sound that it takes me a second to realize is laughter.

"Don't laugh, please." Mortification rises inside me. "I know this may seem like it's coming out of nowhere, but I heard these two women talking today, about how the men in your family have a reputation for—"

"I know our reputation," he cuts in, sobering fast. "That's why I wrap it up. Every time. I don't want any part of that reputation. I don't want to leave a trail of fatherless kids behind me, and I'm not even close to being ready to be a dad."

"I totally understand." I lift my palms, showing him I have nothing to hide. "And I'm not asking you to a be a dad. I would raise the baby on my own. And maybe someday I will marry, and the baby will have a father, but I'm tired of waiting for Mr. Right to make my dreams come true. I'm running out of time. I have to make my own dreams come true, and I want to be a mother more than I've ever wanted anything. And I would be a good one. I would love that child enough to make up for not having a father in the picture, I swear I would."

"I'm sure you would." He drags a clawed hand through his hair. "But this isn't about what kind of mom you would be, Emma. It's about this being...crazy. I mean, I can't even get my head around it."

I swallow past the lump rising in my throat. "That's the first time you've ever said my name."

"Yeah, well, I'm sorry about that." He sounds truly apologetic. "I'm sorry I've been giving you shit and being an asshole."

"Thanks," I say, tears rising in my eyes no matter how hard I try to fight them.

"Seriously, it was nothing personal, I just... Oh God, don't cry." He reaches out, laying a warm hand on my shoulder. "Please, don't cry. There's no reason to cry."

I nod, but my face crumples anyway. "Sorry. I'm just so embarrassed. That was a hard question to ask."

"I know. I mean, I can imagine. Hell, come here." He pulls me in for a hug, and I bury my face in his sweet-smelling flannel while he runs a soothing hand up and down my back.

It feels so nice it makes me cry even harder.

It's been so long since someone touched me in a way that feels nice. I've been so lonely since Jeremy and I broke up. Since months before, really, when he started pulling away, distancing himself from our relationship as he started investing heavily in the bank of Jeremy and Veronica.

"It's fine," Dylan murmurs as I continue to sniffle. "You don't have to be embarrassed. We can pretend this never happened."

"Really?" I squeak.

"Absolutely. I'm good at keeping promises, too. And if I promise to forget this conversation, then it's forgotten. Word of honor. Okay?"

"Okay." I regain control as his hand shifts to a circling motion between my shoulder blades. "But I still won't be able to look you in the eye for at least six months. Maybe a year."

"Well...what if I tell you something embarrassing?" he asks after a beat. "Or at least something I would prefer you didn't know?"

I nod with my cheek still pressed against his chest, relishing the powerful feel of his body through the soft fabric, taking my comfort where I can get it since I know it will probably be a long time before I get a hug from anyone else. "Yes, please."

His hand goes still as he says, "Every time I run into you when you're wearing your glasses, I have to spend a good ten minutes fighting off inappropriate thoughts."

Surprised, I look up, but all I can see is the bottom of his chin. "What kind of inappropriate thoughts?"

He glances down. "Thoughts about how much I'd like for you to shush me at the library, then take me back to your librarian's office and let me apologize in private for being too loud."

My eyes widen, shock banishing the last of my sniffles. "You have dirty librarian fantasies about me?"

His grin is strained, embarrassed, and one of the most charming things I've ever seen. "I do. I'm sorry."

"Don't be sorry," I say, lips curving as I confess, "I've noticed how nice you look in jeans. Even before I considered the...other thing."

"Yeah, the other thing." His focus shifts from my eyes to my mouth. "You don't want me for that job, anyway. I'm way too grouchy."

"You're grouchy during sex?"

His eyes darken. "No. Just in general. Could be

something that's passed down in the DNA, and you don't want a grouchy kid."

"I'm okay with grouchy," I say, a ribbon of hope threading through me. "Everyone's grouchy sometimes. I just want a baby, Dylan. Grouchy or sweet, short or tall, boy or girl, I don't care." I lean into him, pulse leaping as my breasts press against his chest, and his jaw clenches in response. "I know it's a lot to ask, but it wouldn't have to be weird unless we let it be weird. And I'm perfectly willing to play librarian, if that's something you're interested in."

"Now you're playing dirty, Blondie," he says, but the nickname doesn't sound teasing this time.

It sounds like a warning, a promise that if I keep pushing, something is going to give.

But that's just what I want.

So I smile and say, "No, not playing dirty yet, but that can be arranged."

Dylan pulls in a breath and lets it out long and slow, eyes blazing into mine. I can almost see the devil and angel going at it on his shoulders, each one giving their case everything they've got.

Now all I have to do is make sure the angel is the one that wins. Because this truly would be a mission of mercy, a priceless gift I would be oh-so-thankful for.

I press onto tiptoe, bringing my mouth closer to Dylan's as I say, "Don't answer now. Take your time, think it over, and make the decision that feels right. But just know that I would be so very grateful for your help."

I lean in, intending to press a kiss to his cheek, but

he shifts his head at the last moment, and my lips brush his. The second we touch—soft skin on soft skin, breath mingling in the air between us—sparks ignite. Lightning flashes. Thunder rolls. And I'm pretty sure a hole is torn in the space-time continuum.

At least for me.

I don't know if it's the fact that I haven't kissed anyone in seven months or how desperately I want Dylan's help or something magical in the light of the harvest moon, but the moment our lips make contact, I go from definitely interested to dying-for-more-of-Mr.-Hunter at the speed of light.

He threads his hand into my hair and makes a fist, sending my ponytail holder flying as he pulls me in hard and close, kissing me like a drowning man surfacing for a gasp of air. His tongue sweeps through my mouth, stroking, tasting, laying claim as I respond with the same hunger.

I twine my arms around his neck and press closer, as close as two people can get while still fully dressed. I rub against him, relishing the feel of his firm body and the even firmer length growing thick and heavy behind the fly of his jeans.

He wants me, wants *this*.

All I need to do is convince him there's no reason not to take what he wants.

"You feel so good," I murmur between kisses, moaning as his hands grip my ass, pulling me tight to where he's so deliciously hard.

"We should stop," he says, even as he guides my leg

up around his thigh, the better to grind against me exactly where I want him most.

I gasp at the sudden intimacy of the contact, but God, it feels so good. "Oh no, don't stop."

"If I don't stop soon, I'm going to take you right here." His hand roams up to cup my breast through my sweatshirt. "On the ground, in the dirt. It's been a long time for me, Blondie."

"Me, too. Way too long." I moan against his lips as he rolls my nipple through my clothes.

"Then we both know this isn't the way to make this decision." He brings his hands back to my hair, guiding it out of my eyes and then holding my face captive as he stares down at me, breathing fast. "So we're going to go home. Alone. And we'll talk about this tomorrow."

"I was enjoying not talking," I say, my nerves humming and my panties damp with how much I want this.

Want *him*.

I knew from the moment I laid eyes on Dylan Hunter that he was a sexy beast, but I had no idea the chemistry between us would be this combustible. I hadn't known chemistry like this existed. Even with Jeremy, it was never like this.

Like a drug. A high. A fix I want so bad I'm shaking with it.

"Me, too." The hunger that flashes across Dylan's features as his hands return to my back, his fingertips tracing my spine, assures me I'm not alone. "So why don't we put the baby-making talk on hold and go back to my place? I have condoms."

I'm tempted—God, am I tempted—but I wasn't lying when I said I want a baby more than anything. I truly do.

Even more than I want to be naked with this sexy-as-hell man.

"As much as I would love to," I say, "truly. That's not the kind of relationship I need right now. If you decide you don't want to help me, I'll completely understand. But if you won't, I'll need to find someone who will, and that'll be easier if I'm not already involved."

Dylan's eyes narrow, but his mouth remains soft, and after a moment he steps away with a nod. "All right. I'll have an answer for you by tomorrow afternoon. Monday morning at the latest."

Heart lifting, soaring into the air on wings of hope, a smile explodes across my face. "Perfect! Thank you so much. I appreciate you giving this a chance. Some thought. Some time." I wave a hand, awkward again now that there's physical distance between us. "All those things. I appreciate them."

He shakes his head slowly as he backs away. "I still think it's crazy," he warns. "And I'm probably going to say no."

I press my lips together and nod, but secretly I'm thinking, *But maybe you won't say no. Maybe you'll say yes. You're at least going to think about it, which you weren't going to do before we kissed.*

The thought gives me an idea, a naughty, not-playing-fair idea that keeps me smiling as I wave goodbye and Dylan steps through the gate at the edge of his pasture, starting up the hill toward his place.

I have a secret weapon now, something I can use to my advantage if I dare to bend the rules. Honor is all well and good, but this is a battle I'm determined to win at any cost.

Mind made up, I hurry back to where the harvest is well underway, helping Bart shift the light cart as the workers move methodically down the rows to the far side of the vineyard. But inside I'm already at that meeting with Dylan tomorrow, plotting, planning, scheming the best way to play my ace and make sure he has no choice but to say yes.

CHAPTER 4

*N*o. The answer has to be no.

I'm crazy to have even said I would *think* about it. There is *no* answer but *no*. Yes isn't an option. I should have drawn a line in the sand last night and made sure Emma understood I never meant to step over it.

Never.

No matter how sweet her mouth tastes or what an insanely hot kisser she is or how good it felt to have her curvy body pressed tight and grinding against my cock through our clothes.

God, she was hot…

Five-alarm hot…

Wild, hungry, and so much more responsive than I'd imagined she would be.

And *yes*, I've imagined what it would be like to kiss her, imagined Emma's smart mouth melting beneath mine as I show her how much fun we could have if we stopped duking it out for a piece of land that should rightfully be mine. And yes, the real Emma is even more irresistible than the fantasy.

But that's exactly why I should say no. She's the kind of woman it would be so easy to get hooked on, and neither one of us is looking for a steady date.

She wants a no-strings-attached baby, and I want a clear path to a future that's truly mine, not more connections and obligations. Even assuming Emma and I end up hating each other by the time our fucking-for-a-baby experiment is through, there's no way I would be able to live next door to my own child and pretend he's just the neighbor's boy.

I don't want a kid at this point, but if my son were growing up across the pasture, I would want to be a part of his life. I would want to be there when he needed me, especially when he got old enough to wonder why his father wasn't in the picture. I would want to make sure he knew it wasn't because of any flaw in his design; it's just grown-up bullshit, pure and simple.

"Bullshit, bullshit, bullshit," I grumble as I toss plates onto the long wooden table in the front dining room.

"In good spirits this morning, I see." Tristan slams the front door behind him and tosses his jean jacket onto the pile of coats on the bench in the hall. "Rafe up yet?"

"No idea." I open an arm to pull my little half-brother in for a quick hug, before motioning him toward the silverware lying in a tangle at the far end of the table. "He didn't come home last night."

Tristan snorts and shakes his head. "One day back in

town and he already found a woman willing to put up with his ass?"

"At least for the night," I say, earning a grin from Tris. It's crazy how much he looks like Rafe when he smiles—same mile-wide grin and dancing brown eyes—but they couldn't be more different.

Tris is the family do-gooder, the kid who was always saving wounded animals and looking out for the underdog growing up. Rafe is our rebel, blazing his own path without giving a good God damn what anyone else has to say about it.

And then there's me, somewhere in the middle, torn between my heart and my head, my personal goals and my family obligations. My dick and the sound knowledge that getting a stranger pregnant is a stupid idea under any circumstances, no matter how sad a woman looks crying in the moonlight, how sweet her mouth tastes, or how long it's been since I got laid.

If I were Tris or Rafe, this decision would have already been made—they don't traffic in middle ground.

Which gives me an idea...

When Rafe stomps in a few minutes later, whistling the jaunty tune of a man who had a *very* good time last night, I decide to go for it.

"Rafe, get in here. I need to ask your and Tristan's advice on something." I prop my hands on a chair as Rafe swaggers in, clapping Tristan on the back in greeting as he says, "Sure, what's on your mind?"

"First, I need you to promise that you won't mention this to anyone else. No one," I emphasize, keeping my volume low. "Not Dad or your friends or anyone else. Especially not anyone in town."

Tristan's expression sobers. "Of course not. Teepee of silence, man."

When we were kids, our oldest brother Deacon—the only kid from Dad's first marriage—built us a teepee outside. It served as our clubhouse and refuge from family drama when Dad and his lady of the moment were in the middle of a dust-up. The teepee was a place where we felt safe to talk about anything, knowing our brothers would never breathe a word of it to the outside world.

So, even though I'm a grown man, I nod and agree, "Teepee of silence." And then I fill them in on what happened last night, leaving out the more intimate parts but making it clear that attraction and sexual compatibility are not part of what I consider the problem in this situation.

By the time I'm finished, Rafe's eyes are saucer-wide and Tristan is wearing his thoughtful poker face, the one I'm sure serves him well managing the board of a non-profit, but which I can see through in a heartbeat.

He thinks I'm crazy, too. They *both* think I'm crazy.

I've finally found something that the two of them agree on, which makes this decision a no-brainer.

"Forget it." I make a shooing motion with both hands as I step away from the table. "Don't even answer. I'll say no. That's it. It's the only rational answer."

"Don't run off," Rafe says as I start into the kitchen, making me pause in the doorway, close enough to hear Dad whistling as he fries bacon. "You wanted to talk, so let's talk. Why did you tell her you would think about it? There has to be a reason."

Tristan nods. "Right. Your first instinct had to be to say no, right? Even with the land on the table." He waits until I nod in confirmation before continuing. "So what changed your mind?"

I shrug uncomfortably. "I don't know. My thoughts were fuzzy there at the end. It was the middle of the night and she's... Well, she's..." I pull in a breath and let it out long and slow, making Rafe laugh.

"I thought she would be," he says. "But just because she's a sexy little number and you've spent the past year monking it up is no reason to go knocking her up. Have some fun together, date, whatever, and put the baby talk off until later. Preferably a day that never comes."

Tristan frowns. "Some people like the idea of having a family someday, V."

"Not Dylan," Rafe says with complete confidence. "Between Dad and watching the boys every time Deacon deploys, he's had enough babysitting for two lifetimes."

He's right.

But he's...*not* right, too.

A few years from now, or if I meet the right woman, I don't know how I'll feel about starting a family. But I do know his solution isn't going to work. "I already suggested taking things slow. She's not up for it. Said she was tempted, but that her first priority is finding a man willing to do the job. If I won't, she's going to keep looking until she finds someone who will."

"Wow." Tristan blinks faster as he crosses his arms,

leaning against the wall by the sideboard where his mother's vintage Italian china is stored, waiting to become a wedding present when he seals the deal with Kim, his girlfriend since high school. He's the only man in our generation who has been able to make a relationship work for more than a year. When he talks, we all tend to listen.

After a beat, he continues, "So, two things are bothering me about this…"

Rafe and I nod, but neither of us interrupts. That's another thing about Tris—he's thoughtful with his words and won't be rushed.

"The first is that I wonder if you might be underestimating how hard it would be to *not* be a part of this child's life," he says carefully.

I shake my head. "I know it would hard. Especially with her and the baby living right next door. I mean, maybe if she were in another city or state or something…"

"Out of sight, out of mind," Rafe agrees. "That would definitely make it easier for me. Not that I would even *consider* something stupid like this."

As I pull a face at Rafe, Tristan continues, "The other thing is that I wonder if you and Emma are both underestimating how this could affect your relationship with each other."

"They don't have a relationship," Rafe says, brows wiggling up and down as he glances my way. "At least, not yet."

"Right," Tristan agrees. "But if they do decide to go for it. Keeping sex and love separate is one thing, but when you're creating a life together..." He shrugs. "Obviously I don't have personal experience, but I imagine that would be pretty emotionally intense."

Rafe grunts. "That's because you've never fucked someone you weren't in love with."

"No, I haven't," Tristan says, not a bit defensive. He's never been the kind to apologize for being a romantic. "So I could have it all wrong. I don't know. It just feels way too complicated for me."

"Me, too," Rafe agrees. "I know it's hard to walk away from big chemistry, but there are plenty of other grapes on the vine, bro. My old dirt-biking friend Deborah, the one who was out wine tasting with Chastity yesterday, is single. She's a fun girl, easy-going, low pressure. I could set you guys up."

"The girl you were with last night's name is Chastity," Tristan observes dryly.

"Yeah." Rafe scrubs his hand across his face, losing the battle against a wicked grin. "God bless parents who name their kids uptight shit. Those girls are always crazy in the sack. I slept maybe fifteen minutes last night."

Tristan rolls his eyes, slashing a finger across his neck as the twins slam through the door and shuffle, still bleary-eyed, toward the table, clearly having enjoyed their one morning to sleep in late while I handled the eggs.

"You can keep talking." Blake yawns magnificently as he gathers an armful of juice glasses from the sideboard to start his Sunday morning family breakfast duties. "I don't care about your old man gossip."

"Yeah, we already know Uncle Rafe didn't come home last night," Jacob calls over his shoulder on his way into the kitchen for the pitchers of water and juice.

"And we know who he was with." Blake's green eyes flash with mischief as he circles the table, setting out glasses. "Chastity's little sister, Honor, is in our class. She posted a status update saying she was having a hard time sleeping last night, what with all the moaning and groaning coming from her sister's room."

Tristan's nose scrunches. "Seriously, Rafe? You were at this girl's family's house?"

"No, I was at her place," Rafe says. "I didn't know her little sister was sleeping over until I came downstairs this morning and she was sitting there watching TV. But she's seventeen; it's not like she's a kid."

"Yeah," Blake agrees, grinning harder. "She knew what all the 'Oh yes, oh yes, oh yes, Rafe! Rafe!' was about."

While Rafe grabs Blake in a headlock, knuckling his hair, and Tristan expresses further concern that seventeen is too young to be exposed to the sounds of loud, raunchy sex, I head into the kitchen to start bringing in the food. Squeezing past Jacob on his way out with a tray loaded with pitchers, I circle around Dad. He's fishing bacon out of the frying pan with a fork, adding to an already impressively piled-up plate beside him.

"Pancakes and toast are ready, right?" I ask, giving my hands a quick wash at the sink.

"Everything's ready except the bacon." He adds another layer of meat to his already hot pan. "And that'll be up in just a few."

"Sweet. I'll bring everything else out and tell the boys to go ask Pete and Jose if they want to eat with us." If it's a busy day, our farmhands don't take off for our midmorning Sunday meal, but with the hops already in and autumn coming on fast, there's less to do around the property than there was even a month ago.

"I already told Jacob to go fetch Pete and Jose." Dad turns to face me, revealing his "Cereal Killer" apron. "Why don't you hang here with me a minute, son?"

Brows lifting, I lean back against the sink, drying my hands. "Okay. What's on your mind?"

Dad only calls me "son" when he's got something serious to discuss. I just hope he's not planning to lay on another guilt trip about ripping out the vineyards. After sleeping barely three hours last night, I'm not in the mood to defend myself for pulling the family back from the brink of financial ruin.

"My knees and my ticker aren't what they used to be," Dad says, motioning toward his chest with his greasy fork. "But the ears work just fine."

I sigh as I cross my arms, bracing myself for confrontation. "So you heard?"

"I heard, and I've got an opinion, too, if you don't mind taking a second to hear it. Your brothers gave you solid advice, but neither of them has ever been a father."

"All right." I nod, jaw clenched. I'd rather not hear Dad's baby-making advice—I already know we're on opposite sides of that issue—but he's the parent who has always been there for me. He visited us in Mendocino when I was little, and when my mom flaked, he took

47

over raising me without a second of hesitation, even though it cost him his marriage to Francesca.

He's earned the right to preach his truth and have me listen, but that doesn't mean I'm going to take him seriously.

"The way I see it is this." Dad glances out the window over my shoulder, toward Emma's vineyards. "That woman wouldn't have asked for this kind of help unless she was at the end of her rope. Brave new modern world or not, most women still want to have babies with someone they love. Someone they can share the ups and downs with. Being a single parent is a hard gig."

"I can imagine," I say.

Dad nods. "Anyone with sense can. And Emma's a smart cookie. She knows what she's asking for, and I would bet this farm she's willing to do whatever it takes to get you to say yes. Even if it means moving out of state like you were talking about."

My stomach cramps, the thought of asking Emma to leave the land she just settled into this summer banishing my bacon-inspired hunger. "I can't do that. Can you imagine how much money she would lose if she tried to resell that fast?"

"Maybe she doesn't care," Dad says with a shrug. "Maybe it would be worth it to her. You don't know how women get when they're desperate to have a baby. It's like they're possessed, son, and a possessed woman is willing to do all kinds of things that might seem irrational to a guy who just wants to get his rocks off."

He turns back to his bacon, tossing his last words

over his shoulder. "And then you'd have Stroker's land and me out of your hair. His place isn't fancy, but it's plenty big enough for an old bachelor. Two old bachelors if he decides he doesn't want to move to Florida after all."

"I don't want you out of my hair, Dad." *I just want you off my ass*, I add silently, *but I'm not willing to sell myself like a stallion put out to stud to make it happen.*

I decide right then that my answer will be no. The fact that Pop is the only one on board with this plan underlines how insane it is.

I'll do my best to let Emma down easy, wish her the best of luck finding someone to knock her up, and life will go back to normal around here.

Normal. With no heart-stopping kisses in the moonlight, no beautiful woman begging me to take her wherever, whenever I want her—as long as I do it bare.

Bare. I've never fucked a woman bare…

Ever.

And damned if that isn't what I think about the rest of the day, unable to get the thought out of my mind no matter how hard I try, proving that "no" isn't going to be easy to deliver.

CHAPTER 5

FROM THE TEXTS OF EMMA AND CARRIE
HAVERFORD

*E*mma: You got a second? I need a second opinion on this outfit...
sends image file

CARRIE: Holy shit. What are you wearing?! And where have you been hiding those ta-tas? I didn't realize you had that much cleavage! Da-yum!

Small animals could get lost in there, Em.

Have you checked your breasts for chipmunks?

Squirrels?

A litter of stray kittens?

And more importantly, are you sure you meant to send this sext to your little sister?

EMMA: Ha, ha, you're hysterical, as usual, but I'm in a hurry.

And yes, I meant to send it to you! I told you, I need feedback.

Is it too much? Do I look ridiculous? Should I change before he gets here?

CARRIE: He, huh? Tell me more!

I'm guessing he's not your usual boring business douche if he's hot for teacher.

EMMA: I'm supposed to be a librarian.

He's got a thing for librarians…

CARRIE: OH MY GOD. YOU'RE ROLE PLAYING WITH YOUR NEW GUY ALREADY AND YOU HAVEN'T EVEN TOLD ME YOU'RE DATING AGAIN? What's wrong? Do you hate me? Are you still mad because I said your new home smelled like poop?

EMMA: It only smelled like poop for TWO DAYS, Carrie, because we were spreading compost on the new raised beds I put in for the winter garden.

CARRIE: I'll believe it when I smell it…

.   .   .

EMMA: Then come up for a visit next weekend, Miss Fussy Pants, because it smells lovely here today. And the next time we fertilize the garden, I'm going to have Bart get compost from the organic nursery down the street. Their compost doesn't smell like poop at all, which is the way it should be assuming you've got the proper carbon-to-nitrogen ratio.

CARRIE: The amount of farmer stuff you've learned is really impressive. Boring, but impressive. I'm proud of you. And I'm glad you're loving your stinky new life.

EMMA: I am loving it, but I'm going to love it more if I can convince my new friend that we should be special friends, so can I get some outfit feedback please? Is he going to laugh at me? Or think I'm trying too hard?

CARRIE: Okay, wait, back this up. You're not special friends yet?

EMMA: No. He's thinking about it and is going to give me his decision today.

CARRIE: WHAT? Fuck him! What's to think about?
You are a smoking hot pixie vixen with giant boobs! And you're intelligent, successful, sweet, funny, and

probably the most generous person I've ever met. I mean, who deliberately locks themselves away with a bunch of sticky-fingered kids every weekend to teach them life skills for free?

EMMA: Lots of people. Some of us actually enjoy the company of children. And teaching them new things.

CARRIE: Gross.

EMMA: Lol. You don't mean that. I've seen you at book signings. You are SO sweet to your readers.

CARRIE: That's because my readers are intelligent children who recognize quality entertainment. They've set themselves apart from the mouth-breathers with their imagination and excellent taste in literature.

EMMA: So humble. As always.

CARRIE: Yeah, well, we all have our glitches, don't we?

I think too highly of myself and you don't think nearly highly enough.

Seriously, show this guy the door, Em. Better yet, don't even let him in. Take off your sexy outfit and save it for someone who will appreciate what an honor it is to spend time with an all-around amazing person like you.

EMMA: It's not like that, Carrie. It's complicated in a way I don't have time to explain right now because he's going to be here in ten minutes.

So PLEASE just tell me if this is the kind of thing that might scare a man away.

We did kiss last night so I know he's attracted to me.

And he told me that my glasses make him have naughty librarian fantasies, so this isn't something I pulled out of thin air.

But maybe I'm better off playing it safe?

Just in case he says no?

If he says no while I'm wearing jeans and a sweater, it will be much less embarrassing than having to slink away in a skin-tight pencil skirt and my cleavage shirt.

CARRIE: So it's the shirt that's doing all that? Where did you get it, if you don't mind me asking? I've got a hot date tomorrow night.

EMMA: CARRIE PLEASE!! I'M RUNNING OUT OF TIME TO CHANGE CLOTHES!

. . .

CARRIE: Okay, okay! No, don't change! Stay the way you are and own the shit out of it, because you look smoking hot.

EMMA: Are you sure?

CARRIE: Yes, I'm sure. The only reason you're tempted to change is to avoid potential embarrassment, right? And avoiding something that might not even happen is no reason to make a decision.

EMMA: Right. You're absolutely right. Life isn't about minimizing risk; it's about maximizing joy. And sometimes that means jumping for that next rock, even if you end up slipping and falling on your butt in the river in the process.

CARRIE: Exactly! Because you might not fall.
You might land solidly on that rock and ride it all night long...

EMMA: Now who's gross?

. . .

CARRIE: All night long, Em. You deserve it. But first be sure to tell him how disappointed you are in him for returning his library books three days late. ;)

EMMA: I'm going now. I can see him walking across the field. He's on his way!

CARRIE: Shit, are you humping your hottie neighbor?
The one with the sexy hair and the Brad Pitt mouth?!!!

EMMA: I'm not humping anyone yet. So let me go and stop making me nervous!
I can't believe you even remember him.
You barely exchanged two words with the man.

CARRIE: That's not the kind of fine-ass farmer you forget. But you're not the kind of woman a guy forgets, either. You've got this. Go get him, baby! No fear.

EMMA: No fear!
wide-eyed emoji
biting fingernails emoji
book emoji
stiletto emoji

CHAPTER 6

DYLAN

*A*ll the way across the field, through the gate, and up the path to Emma's place, I'm mentally rehearsing what I'm going to say to take the sting out of this rejection. The last thing I want to do is hurt her feelings or her pride. I already feel like a jackass for giving her such a chilly welcome to the neighborhood. Holding her while she cried last night changed everything between us. And then kissing her like I was going to fuck her standing up with all our clothes on changed it some more.

I have to tread carefully. Wisely. Respectfully.

I jog up the front steps to rap on the door of the two-hundred-year-old farmhouse she's spruced up with a fresh paint job and dozens of brightly potted plants scattered across the porch. There are two red rocking chairs at the far end, too.

I'm thinking that might be a good place to have a friendly conversation—nothing more soothing than a rock in a rocking chair, preferably with a beer—when the door swings open and my cock springs to attention so fast it's like someone pulled the emergency switch in the erection-center of my brain.

And that someone is this woman, in a skin-tight pencil skirt, sky-high red heels, and a white shirt that's unbuttoned far enough to reveal the twin swells of the most beautiful breasts I've ever seen. Touching her through her sweater last night, I could tell she was a tempting handful, but this is the first time I've seen all that creamy, luscious flesh on display.

Add in her red wire-rim glasses and the blond hair piled in a messy knot on top of her head, and I'm a goner.

Gone. Completely gone. So out of it I don't remember stepping through the door, only coming back to my senses as Emma closes it behind me.

I'm losing it, fast, everything I planned to say evaporating in the rush of lava dumping into my bloodstream.

"Hi," Emma says, her fingers playing with a button on her shirt. The top button, the one that—if undone— would send her breasts spilling free.

Vivid images of my fingers on that button, my mouth on her breasts, my hands cupping her fullness as my tongue plays back and forth across her nipples, making her moan, flash on my mental screen. My blood pressure skyrockets, and my throat squeezes tight. Even if I could think of something to say right now, I wouldn't be able to get the words out.

"I was taking care of a few things in my office when you called. Why don't we talk in there." Emma motions with a smile for me to follow her and starts across the room.

I hesitate, watching the swivel of her hips, observing the way the light gray fabric strains across the firm roundness of her spectacular ass.

Fuck me.

Now all I can think about is my fingers sliding beneath the hem, guiding her skirt up and over her thighs, baring her gorgeous backside to my hands, my mouth. In my imagination, I already have her bent over her desk and my tongue is making intimate friends with her pussy.

I need to get out of here. Now.

I should call after her and tell her I'll wait for her on the porch. Then I should head back outside, sit down in a rocker, and do whatever it takes to talk my cock down from this hard-on that's making my jeans feel like a medieval instrument of torture.

Instead, I follow her into her office, a bright space with bookshelves on three of the four walls and a view of the valley on the far side of her property. I deliberately leave the door open behind me, hands balling into fists at my sides as Emma turns to face me, leaning back against the edge of a desk that's plenty big enough to accommodate any number of getting-it-on-in-the-office fantasies.

No. You will not bend; you will not break. You will stay strong, deliver the bad news, and get out of here as fast as humanly possible.

"Would you like something to drink?" Emma asks, fingering that damned button again. *Curse* that button.

"I have coffee or tea in here, or I can get iced tea from the kitchen if you'd rather have something cool."

I definitely need something to help me cool off, but iced tea isn't going to do the job, so I shake my head. "No thanks. I've got a lot of bookkeeping to take care of this afternoon, myself. I just wanted to have a quick talk with you in person, make sure you understood where I was coming from."

Worry creeps into her delicate features. "Okay."

My breath rushing out, I fix my gaze on the green-hooded lamp on her desk, the better to get through this without being distracted by how sexy she looks. "I did a lot of thinking last night, and this morning, and I—"

"I did some thinking, too," she cuts in, fingers threading together in front of her as she stands. "And I looked over my records."

"Your records," I echo with a frown.

"Yes." She nods as she moves closer. "And according to those records you have six overdue books, Mr. Hunter. And that's not something I take lightly in my library."

I realize what she's up to and shake my head. "I'm sorry, Emma, I don't—"

"So what should I do with you, Mr. Hunter?" She stops in front of me, close enough for me to catch the lavender and honey of her perfume and the sugar-smoke Emma scent I became intimately acquainted with last night.

I can still taste her—hot, sexy, and salty sweet.

God help me, all I want is another taste. I want it so bad I know the chances of getting out of here without violating the boundaries I mentally put in place are getting slimmer with every passing moment.

Still, I try. "I can't play games with you, Blondie. That's what I came to tell you."

"This isn't a game." Her expression is as serious as the heart attack she's about to give me when she lays a hand on my arm. "Have you even read those books? Do you understand how long the waiting list is for those particular titles? They're very popular, Mr. Hunter, some of the *best* stories this library has to offer."

"I don't read fiction." I gaze down at her, keenly aware of how close her lips are to mine. "Biographies, memoirs, non-fiction. That's it."

"Why?" she murmurs, the curve of her breast brushing against my chest, making my jaw clench and my already swollen cock pulse. "Don't you enjoy pretend?"

"I haven't had much time for pretend," I find myself confessing, all my defenses now devoted to keeping my hands to myself.

"Then why don't we make time?" Her palm skims up to my shoulder, and before I make a conscious decision to move, my arms are around her waist.

Because my body is a traitor to my cause and has zero interest in walking out of Emma's office before this game is through.

CHAPTER 7

DYLAN

"*T*here's nothing pretend about what I want to do to you right now, Librarian Haverford." My voice is low and rough as I cup her ass, drawing her close to where I'm so fucking hard for her.

Her breath catches and her lips part. "And what's that, Mr. Hunter? How do you intend to get back into the library's good graces?"

"How about I make you come on my mouth?" I mold my fingers to her ribs, letting them hover beneath her breast as I brush my thumb over that demon button. "After I kiss every inch of you."

Emma's lids droop to half-mast as she tilts her head back. "That sounds like an incredible place to start."

"An incredible place to finish," I correct. "I'm not up for anything more."

Humming softly, she runs her hand over my erection through my jeans, drawing a groan from low in my throat. God, I want her hands on me. Her mouth on me. Her pussy slick and tight around my cock as I take her right here on the floor of her office, but I'm not willing to lie to her to get what I want.

"No baby-making," I add, to ensure we're perfectly clear. "If we have sex, we're using a condom."

She leans in as she shakes her head, brushing her lips gently against mine. "That wasn't the deal."

"Come on, Blondie." I drag my knuckle back and forth over her tight nipple through the thin fabric of her shirt. "It's clear we both want this. Want it pretty fucking bad if we can't keep our hands off of each other for more than five minutes. So why don't you let me make you feel good without the strings attached." I pinch her taut flesh between my fingers, drawing a soft moan from her pretty lips. "I might be a bad library patron, but I'm going to excel at making you come, sweetheart. I promise."

"I believe you." Her nails dig into the skin at the back of my neck, making me desperate to feel them raking across my bare shoulders while I'm moving inside her, driving her crazy. "But my one condition is non-negotiable. No condoms. If that's something you can't handle, then we should stop now."

Stop.

It's a horrible idea, the worst word I've ever heard. It makes me physically ill to even consider such a terrible, awful, shitty, no-good thing.

I don't want to stop, I want to go and keep going until there is no part of this woman that's a mystery to me. Until I've marked every inch of her skin with my lips, my tongue, my teeth dragging across the inside of her thigh, at her elegant neck, across the pink tips of her breasts and the pinker slickness between her legs.

But I'm a grown man, and my head is calling the shots around here, not my dick.

And so, drawing from the deep reserves of self-control that have kept me calm and steady through every crisis my family has faced the past few years, I capture Emma's wrists gently in my hands, draw her arms from around my neck, and take a head-clearing step back.

"Oh no." Her breath rushes out as her brow furrows sadly. "We're really stopping? I don't want to stop."

"Me, either." I swallow hard, fighting to keep my eyes from drifting below her neck. "But I can't do what you want. It would be too hard to live next door to my kid and not be a part of his or her life. I'm not ready to be a father, but if the baby's right here, under my nose, I don't think—"

"Then I can move. After. If it works." The words bursting from her kiss-swollen mouth are so close to what I need to hear that my resolve wavers.

Still, I do my best to be the voice of reason. "You just got settled. You don't want to pull up stakes and start over again. Think of how much money that will cost, let alone the time and frustration involved in—"

"I don't care about the money." She stands up straighter, her chin lifting. "If money were my top priority, I would never have left Silicon Valley and the job that was killing me. I want to do *something* I love, and share my life with *someone* I love. I can make wine in lots of places. This might be my only shot at a baby."

My teeth dig into my bottom lip as I fight for control. "I've never gotten a woman pregnant before, Emma. Yes, the men in my family have a reputation, but that doesn't mean—"

"A well-earned reputation," she cuts in. "I'm willing to take a chance on that. My ex and I tried for eight months without any luck, Dylan. Clearly I need super sperm to break through the fertility barrier."

"Maybe it was him." If I'm even going to *consider* changing my mind, I need to make damned sure she understands what she's getting in exchange for uprooting her entire life. "Did you get tested to see which of you might have a problem?"

Emma's features go still as her gaze shifts to the thick flowered rug beneath our feet. "No, but I know it's me."

"Without a test, I don't see how you—"

"Jeremy's new fiancée is pregnant," she says. "Eight months along."

I wince. "And you two broke up..."

"Seven months ago," she says, lips curving in a humorless smile. "Right after he told me he'd been cheating and Veronica was having his baby."

"Bastard," I murmur softly, wanting to pull her in for a hug but knowing better. I can't trust myself to touch her. Not yet. Not while I'm still so hard it feels like my cock has caught some exotic fever that isn't going to end well for either of us.

So I settle for a firm, "He didn't deserve you."

Emma glances up, big blue eyes creasing at the edges. "Thanks. But honestly, I'm not upset about it anymore. If he hadn't betrayed me, I don't know if I would have had the courage to stop betraying myself. This new life and everything I love about it is because of what he did."

"No, it's because of you," I say, hating to see her ex getting credit for her bravery. "You've got giant balls, Blondie."

Her nose wrinkles. "Thank you, I guess. Though I would rather have giant ovaries. Or at least ovaries that work better than mine. I have endometriosis, so that's part of the fertility issue." She shrugs, the motion causing her breasts to bounce lightly, making my mouth go dry all over again. "Chances are we could have three months of fun together and there would be no baby."

"And what's your plan if that happens?" I ask, tone cautious, though temptation is hitting me hard.

"I don't know. Most likely fertility treatments and a sperm donor..." She pushes her glasses higher on her nose with a sniff. "But I'm not thinking that far ahead just yet. I've learned you can only look so far into the future before it becomes a waste of energy and resources. Nine times out of ten, it's better to live in the now."

In the now...

Right now, all I want to do is kiss her. Touch her. Slide inside her without a barrier between my cock and a woman for the first time and see if it's as good as it's rumored to be.

And why shouldn't I if she's really willing to leave town if I manage to get her knocked up? I won't miss a kid I've never met, she'll have the baby she wants more than anything, Stroker's land will be mine, and all will be right with the world.

There's only one thing standing in my way, "If we do this…"

Emma's eyes light up like it's Christmas and she just spotted everything she ever wanted—and a baby unicorn—under the tree.

"*If* we do this," I repeat, holding up a warning finger, "you have to make me a promise."

Her head bobs fast. "Yes. Of course. Name it."

"If anything ever happens to the kid and you need a blood donation or a kidney or something only a biological father can give, you reach out. Let me know."

Confusion dulls the joy illuminating her features. "Really? You would do that? For a child you've never even met?"

"There are some responsibilities you can't abdicate, even if you might want to."

"I'm sure most sperm donors feel differently," she says, head cocking thoughtfully. "But I can see where you're coming from. And it makes me even more certain that I picked the right person. Your heart's in a good place, Dylan."

My breath rushes out in a strained laugh. "You wouldn't say that if you knew all the dirty things I've been imagining since you answered the door in that outfit."

Her eyes narrow as her lips curve. "Oh yeah? Things like what?"

"Things like you bent over your desk," I say, voice

low. "While I lift that skirt up over your hips and see what you're wearing underneath."

"Or what I'm *not* wearing." The words are enough to make my head spin as every ounce of blood in my body surges to my cock.

I'm seconds from turning her around, jerking up that skirt, and calling her bluff, when a knock on the doorframe behind me makes us both jump.

"Sorry to bother you, Em." It's Bart, Emma's vineyard manager. "But the couple who bought the winemaker tour at the charity auction is here."

Emma makes a distressed sound as she turns to glance at a clock on one of the bookshelves. "But they're not supposed to arrive until four."

Bart shakes his head. "I know, but they're here now, and they apparently drove all the way from the city. I didn't want to tell them to head into town to kill two hours without consulting you first."

Emma sighs. "No, of course. Thank you, Bart. I don't want them to have to wait. Tell them I'll be out in ten minutes, as soon as I change." She sounds about as thrilled as I feel. "And ask Neil to get them started with a glass of Sauvignon Blanc, please? Something to take the edge off after their drive?"

"Will do," Bart says, lifting a hand to me as he turns to go. "Thanks again for the help last night, Dylan. You saved our asses."

"My pleasure," I say, but the truth is my pleasure has just been cut off at the pass.

Or at least postponed for far longer than I would

like, considering I'm dying to take Emma right here, right now, hot and fast up against the wall.

But that's not how this is playing out, and it's probably for the best. No matter how unconventional our arrangement is going to be, we should probably get to know each other a little better before we get naked and horizontal.

Or vertical, or any other positions my naughty librarian has in mind...

"I'm so sorry," Emma says as soon as we're alone. "Can we meet up later? Same place, same librarian outfit, maybe around five o'clock?"

"Why don't we meet for dinner in town, instead?" I hate to pass up the librarian play, but we're more likely to have a rational conversation if we meet in a place where we won't be alone. "Domenica's? Six o'clock? That'll give us both time to wrap up work, and then we can grab food and get to know each other better before picking up where we left off."

A smile lights her face. "Sounds perfect. See you at six."

"At six," I echo, already knowing that the next four hours will drag by at a snail's pace. But soon, oh-so-soon, I'm going to know what's it like to have Emma every dirty way we want each other.

And no matter how crazy this is...

I can't fucking wait.

CHAPTER 8

EMMA

I can't remember the last time I was this excited for a date.

Even though this *isn't* a date, I keep reminding myself. It's just food before sex.

Before wild, hot, no-holds-barred, *baby-making* sex.

Dylan and I are really going to do it! We're going biking without a helmet, sky-diving without a parachute. Except that instead of having a horrible accident or plummeting to our deaths, there might be a baby at the end of our time together.

Maybe even by the end of tonight...

Just the thought of it is enough to make my heart race and my entire body flush with anticipation. Who knew trying to conceive could be so sexy? Back when Jeremy and I were trying, the sex was good, but I never felt anything like this giddy, spastic, about-to-burst-with-excitement feeling that's had my head spinning all day long.

Even while giving the early-bird Parsons—lovely

couple, terrible timing—their tour, I had to fight the urge to burst out into a spontaneous dance party or shout something highly inappropriate like, "Get out of my way, bitches, mama's going to get some tonight!"

Yes, it's been seven months since I got laid, so I'm sure that's part of what has me feeling floatier than a bottle of pinot for dinner, but most of it is just...Dylan.

Dylan, who kisses with a single-minded intensity that leaves no doubt he's going to be the best lover I've ever had. Dylan, who looks at me like he wants to devour me whole, in one ravenous gulp, making me feel so sexy and desired that I don't stress about what I should wear to dinner. No matter what it is, Dylan is going to want to rip it off of me and make love all night long.

No, not make love. Make a baby, make whoopee, make a trip to Intercourse, Pennsylvania. Love has nothing to do with what you and Dylan are going to get up to in your bed tonight.

"And that's just fine," I tell my reflection as I smooth on a coat of lipstick and head out the door to grab my bike.

I have nothing to be ashamed of. I'm a grown woman, making a grown woman's decision. I'm not a hussy or a harlot or an unlovable loser because I'm treating sex like a business arrangement for once in my life. Besides, it's not like either Dylan or I are doing something we don't want to do, just for the sake of babies or land. It's clear every time we touch that we're going to enjoy getting naked together *very* much.

Hell, even the eye contact is combustible.

I'm getting off my bike in the back parking lot at Domenica's Italian Roadhouse when Dylan pulls in. I look up, and our gazes collide with enough heat to grill half a dozen artichoke and feta cheese pizzas, and I smile, fighting a laugh as he swings out of his truck and heads my way.

"What's funny, Blondie?" he asks, the sizzle still in his eyes.

"Nothing," I say, then confess in a giddy whisper, "I'm just excited about getting naked with you."

He laughs even as his expression goes from sizzling to smoldering. "Me, too. You always say what's on your mind?"

"Usually," I confess. "My sister says I have poor social skills from spending a decade glued to a computer screen."

"I like your social skills. Pretty excited about getting naked with you, too." He wraps his arm around my waist, leaning down to kiss my cheek before he whispers into my ear, "You look amazing in these jeans, but you're going to look even better out of them. Want to get dinner to go, throw your bike in the back of my truck, and head back to your place? If we talk while we wait for food, that's enough getting to know each other, right?"

I nod, my breath rushing out as my fingers dig lightly into his biceps, those thick, powerful muscles I can't wait to have bared to my touch. "Yes. Food to go is an excellent idea. You're brilliant."

He laugh-growls again as he hugs me closer. "Not

brilliant; suffering. I've been hard for you all day. You're all I could think about."

"Me, too." I take a steadying breath as I pull back to look into his eyes. "It's kind of nice knowing how the night's going to end, isn't it?"

"Very," he agrees. "No games."

"Or stress. Or wondering whether your lace thong is going to be appreciated or you're enduring fabric in uncomfortable places all night long for nothing."

"Lace thong." He curses softly, his jaw muscle clenching tight. "Pizza. To go. Now. Before I toss your fine ass in my truck and take off without provisions."

Fighting another giddy grin—I can't wait to be tossed anywhere he wants to toss me, but I've also barely eaten all day—I start up the paving stone path. Out front, the porch is already filling with people waiting for tables, playing checkers or chess on boards painted on old wine barrels while they wait. We step up to the hostess stand and place our takeout order before staking out a bench to wait by the antique tractor that decorates the front lawn. The hour is early, but the air is already thick with the smell of smoked mozzarella, basil, and Domenica's unique creamy tomato sauce.

Soon, my stomach starts to rumble. Loudly.

Dylan nudges my shoulder with his. "You going to make it fifteen minutes?"

"Maybe." I roll my eyes as my stomach lets out another mournful howl. "Maybe not. If I die from hunger before we get back to my place, I'm going to come back from the dead just to slap myself for forgetting to eat regularly."

Dylan squeezes my hand. "I'll keep you distracted until the pizza gets here. Want to hear a story about that tractor?"

"I would love to hear a story about that tractor. My sister makes fun of me for being a farm nerd, but I enjoyed my tractor class at the junior college. Gave me a new appreciation for farm machinery."

He arches a brow. "Is that right? You can drive a tractor? A city slicker like you?"

"I can drive three different kinds of tractors and dig a ditch with a backhoe." I meet his gaze, narrowing my eyes as I nod. "Yeah, it's okay. You can be impressed. I'm pretty impressive."

"You are," he says with a tip of his head. "I've clearly been underestimating your skills."

"It's okay. I forgive you. Considering you saved my harvest last night and apologized so sweetly for being a jerk and all."

His lips curve into a crooked line. "Yeah, well, I really am sorry about that. It's been a rough couple of years, but that's no excuse for forgetting my manners."

I drop the teasing tone. "I heard about your dad. But the cancer is in remission now? He's doing okay?"

"He's great. Physically." Dylan stretches his arms out along the back of the bench. "But he still hasn't forgiven me for ripping out our vines and planting hops instead. We were grape farmers for over a hundred years. He feels like I betrayed the Hunter family legacy, spit on my ancestors' graves, et cetera."

"But you were just doing what you thought was best, right?"

He sighs. "I was doing what I had to do to keep paying the bills. Our entire vineyard was infected with Pierce disease. Everything had to come out, and it would have taken money and time we didn't have to spare to put disease-resistant vines back in."

"Right, Pierce disease." My cheeks flush. "Bart told me that's why you pulled out the blackberry vines close to my property line. To reduce the chance of Pierce disease spreading to our side of the trail. I owe you an apology for being difficult about that."

He grins that cocky grin of his. "Apology accepted. Just trying to be a good neighbor, Blondie."

"You are a good neighbor." I return his smile. "Every time I run into Mr. Stroker, he always sings your praises. Says you're the grandson he never had."

Dylan grunts with an exaggerated scowl. "But he still agreed to consider your bid, the greedy old bastard. Let's see if he still loves me after I let him haul in that crop alone this year."

"You wouldn't," I say, hoping I'm right. If not, I'll have to hire someone to help the old man. I don't want him getting hurt or losing profits because I started a bidding war.

Dylan rolls his eyes. "Of course I wouldn't. He's eighty-five. If he dropped dead throwing pumpkins onto a flat bed, I'd never forgive myself."

I shake my head, warmth spreading through my chest as I study Dylan's face. "Watch out, Hunter. I'm beginning to think this grumpy exterior of yours is a thin shell covering a sweet, soft, gooey center."

"There's nothing soft or gooey about me, Haverford." He dips his lips closer to mine as he adds, "And I'm going to prove it as soon as I get you alone."

My breath rushes out as another wave of longing surges across my skin to pool between my legs. "How can it take *this* long to cook a pizza?"

"I don't know, but at least we distracted your stomach."

"But you still haven't told me the tractor story." I pat his thigh then leave my hand where it is because— muscles. And more muscles. Holy quadriceps, I can't wait to trace every cut on his phenomenal body with my tongue.

"Sorry, I'm easily sidetracked." He nods toward the tractor. "When my brother Rafe and I were kids, that's the tractor they used to pull the winning float down Main Street during the Harvest Parade. Our 4H club won every year because we were committed to excellence in all things—especially things that bagged you a trophy and attention from girls."

I grin. "You had your priorities in order, is what you're saying."

"Exactly." He nudges my shoulder with his again in a way that warms me all over. It feels like something he would do with a real friend, not just a woman he's going to bang for fun, land, and babies, and I'm starting to think I'd enjoy counting Dylan among my friends. "But when we were in eighth grade, the Russian River Boy Scouts beat us out. Their scout leader was on the judging committee and swung the rest of the sell-outs his way with free tickets to see a monster truck exhibition."

I make a scandalized sound. "Bribes and coercion. That doesn't sound very boy-scoutly to me."

"Not at all," Dylan agrees, warming to his story. "Rafe and I were pissed. So we decided to teach the bastards a lesson."

"You toilet papered the boy scouts' houses?"

"Hell, no," he scoffs. "We had three growing boys in our house back then. We couldn't afford to waste toilet paper. And we were 4H kids, so we were resourceful and knew our way around farm equipment."

"Uh-oh," I say, already seeing where this is going.

He grins. "The night before the parade, we snuck into the garage where they stored the floats and put bleach in the tractor's fuel tank. Come time for the big moment, the tractor wouldn't start, and the Boy Scouts' winning float never got its victory lap down Main Street."

"Served them right. But I'm betting the owner of the tractor wasn't too happy."

"Oh, Mr. Caputo was pissed." Dylan laughs beneath his breath. "Somehow, Dad figured out that Rafe and I were responsible—he always had a sixth sense about shit like that—so he made us mow Caputo's lawn for the next three years for free. Even though the tractor was already ancient, even back then, and probably not worth more than a couple hundred bucks."

"Wow." My eyes go wide. "Three years? That's pretty harsh."

"We would probably still be mowing it for free if Mr. Caputo hadn't moved to Texas. Dad has zero tolerance for destruction of property." He shrugs. "And I'm sure part of it was to keep us too busy to get into trouble. Having two teen boys the same age isn't easy. My nephews have taught me that."

I look up at him, frowning as I bring up a visual of the teen boys I've seen zipping up and down the bike trail on their way to friends' houses. They're identical twins, but Rafe and Dylan certainly aren't. "So, you and Rafe are twins, too? I would *never* have imagined. You're so different."

Dylan's grin takes on a wry edge. "No. We're two months apart."

I draw a blank for a moment before understanding dawns. "Oh. I see. So...different mothers obviously."

"Yeah, my mom was the other woman. I didn't come to live with Pop until I was older, but after that, Rafe and I were pretty much inseparable."

I'm about to ask him if his mother was in the picture at all—a question too intimate for a friend with benefits —when the hostess calls his name, saving me from crossing the line. I'm going to have to be careful. It was easy to keep my emotional distance from grumpy Dylan, who teased the shit out of me. Friendly Dylan, with his dimpled smile and easy way with a story, is another thing entirely.

He bounces to his feet and reaches down to help me up, looking nearly as giddy as I feel. "Let's get the goods and get out, Haverford."

"The sooner the better." I take his hand, a zinging feeling skittering up my arm. "But I'm paying. My treat."

"You're not paying." He snorts at the apparent

ridiculousness of the suggestion. "I'm old-fashioned, Blondie. When we go out, I'm paying."

"Then I guess we'll have to stay in, because I believe in paying my share."

Dylan flashes a heated look over his shoulder. "Staying in is fine, too, princess. More than fine."

That look, the nickname, and all the sexy, sinful things they imply steal my words away, leaving my arms much too limp to wrestle him for the check. He pays, tucks the two pizzas and salad we ordered under one arm, and gathers me close with the other. As we circle around the restaurant to the parking lot, more than a few folks cast curious glances our way, making me wonder if meeting in a public place was a good idea, after all.

I'm not usually shy about people knowing who I'm dating, but this isn't a date, and Dylan and I are going to expire in no more than three months. Maybe sooner.

And then I'll be the city slicker who got dumped by Mercyville's golden boy, because no one will ever believe that *I* dumped him. I'll be an object of pity all over again, just like in my old life, when mutual friends called to commiserate before attending a dinner party hosted by Jeremy and his new girlfriend.

"I encourage you to eat in my truck." Dylan hands me the pizzas then lifts my bike as if it weighs nothing at all and loads it into the back of his truck. "Less time we'll have to spend eating when we get to your place."

"What about you?" I push away my melancholy thoughts. I refuse to sully the beginning of this with thoughts of the end. "Would you like me to shove pizza in your mouth as you drive? I'm ambidextrous, so I can do that."

He laughs. "Thanks, but like I said, I grew up in a house with brothers. I can take down half a pizza on the walk from the truck to your front door."

And amazingly, he does.

And before I know it, we're closing my front door, setting what's left of our dinner on the entry table, and coming together in the dark.

CHAPTER 9

DYLAN

*T*his afternoon, when I was imagining how things would go down between Emma and I tonight, it started out slow, with some bone-melting kisses and me unwrapping her delicious body, piece by piece, pausing to discover, to savor, to taste and tease until she was so hot she was begging me to get her naked faster.

The reality is a whirlwind.

A hurricane.

A brush fire catching and surging out of control.

The second the door closes behind us, we're on each other like starving people. Our mouths crash together and our tongues wage sweet war as we hurry across the living room, tearing off clothes and letting them fall where they may.

For a moment, as we stumble through the door to her bedroom, where pale lamplight illuminates a four-poster bed, I flirt with the idea of slowing down. We could take a beat, take a breath. I could take the wheel and set a more sustainable pace. But before I can act on my good intentions, Emma has stepped out of her jeans and is back in my arms, kissing me like she intends to devour me from the mouth down, and I'm lost.

Lost in her heat, her fire.

Her...other things that are hot that I can't remember right now because her shirt is over her head and her breasts are in my hands, covered by only the thinnest white lace. I'm so close to having her nipples in my mouth it's impossible to think of anything else.

"I want to kiss you here." I brush my thumbs over her tight tips as her knees hit the edge of the mattress.

"Yes, please," she says as I shove my jeans to the floor and she pops the clasp on her bra. I lunge out of my pants, and we tumble to the bed, her pinned beneath me as I draw her bra down her arms then cup her breasts in my hands.

They are twin handfuls of pure feminine softness, topped by pale pink nipples already pulled tight for me. I circle first one with my tongue, and then the other, licking and biting, making her squirm before I suck her deep, tugging with rhythmic pulls until she groans, an abandoned sound that makes my cock throb.

"Yes, oh please." She fists her hands in my hair, hanging on tight as I transfer my attention to her other breast, treating it to the same sweet torture.

I keep at it until she writhes against me, clearly desperate for more. Only then do I slide my hand down the front of her panties.

When I reach that sweet promised land and feel how

ready she is for me, my breath rushes out. "God, Emma, you're so wet."

"I want you so much." She moans against my lips as I kiss her again, fucking her mouth with my tongue as my fingers thrust into her heat.

She spreads her legs wider in response, shamelessly lifting into my hand, giving me a preview of how incredible it's going to be to be inside her. My heart stops for a beat, only to jerk back into motion as she reaches down, rubbing my erection through the thin cotton of my boxer briefs.

"Please, I'm ready." She pushes my underwear lower on my hips, setting my cock free, making my breath catch as her cool hand strokes my fever-hot length. "I've been ready since last night. I'm dying to feel you inside me."

"We don't have to rush," I say, even as I strip my boxers down my legs so fast you would think they were on fire. By the time I've kicked them to the floor, she's wiggled out of her white lace panties, too, revealing the prettiest pussy I've ever seen.

Truly, the absolute prettiest. A total heart-stopper.

I bring trembling hands to her inner thighs, cursing as I take her in by the soft lamp light. She is so delicate, so finely made, and so wet that the salty, sexy heat of her rises all around me, making it impossible to resist the need to get my mouth between her legs.

She gasps as I slide lower on the bed. "Oh, no, I don't usually—"

Before she can finish, I lean in, teasing my tongue through her slickness to circle her clit, and her words end in a sharp inhale. Then a moan. And then a cry of surprised pleasure as I cup her breasts in my hands and angle my mouth, playing with her nipples as I draw my top lip over my teeth and roll the softened hardness over her clit again and again as my tongue strokes deep inside her.

I take her, claim her, prove to her that she can trust me to deliver, to ensure she *never* leaves my bed unsatisfied.

Emma cries out once, twice, before the third cry breaks into a long, low moan-whimper-gasp as her thighs begin to tremble on either side of my face. She comes hard, flooding my mouth with the primal taste of her, making it impossible to hold off another second.

I have to be inside her—now—or I'm going to come the next time she touches me. I surge over her, claiming her mouth as my hand instinctively reaches toward the nightstand.

But we're not at my place, and there is no condom waiting to be rolled on before I slide inside this woman locking her legs around my waist and rocking her slick pussy against my cock. This is all there is—her and me and all the heat raging between us, making me feel like my heart is going to burst as I fit the head of my cock to her entrance.

Gritting my teeth, I pull back, fighting for control as I meet Emma's gaze, muscles clenching tighter as I see her parted lips and glazed eyes. She looks sexy as hell fresh from coming on my mouth. It's all I can manage not to sink into her that very second, but some sickly chivalrous part of me has to make sure, to give her one last chance to change her mind.

"You're sure this is what you want?" I force the words out as a bead of sweat rolls down the side of my face, testimony to how hard I'm working to hold back.

To wait. To resist.

"More than anything," she says, without a hint of doubt. "Inside me, Dylan. Now. Please."

I don't make her ask twice. I push forward, sinking into her, chest aching as her slick heat grips me tight. God, she's so fucking tight. And she feels so insanely good, wild and sensual as she rocks into me, taking every inch of my cock, transporting me to some previously unknown level of carnal heaven.

Sex is almost always good and often great, but this...

This is magic.

This is paradise.

This is going to ruin me for fucking with condoms for the rest of my life.

But I'm too far gone for the realization to bring me down. I'm too busy tasting Emma, feeling her, stroking inside her until she cries out against my mouth and comes for me again, so hard it takes my breath away. From that first contraction, the first clench of her body around my throbbing length, I know I'm a goner.

But instead of pulling out—the way I feared I might if last minute second-thoughts got the better of me—I pump harder, faster, driving into her so deep that as I finally thrust forward, coming with a groan, my balls are pulsing against the seam of her ass.

And then I'm lost, my release hitting so hard I'm no longer in control.

It's like losing traction on black ice. One second I'm behind the wheel, making things happen, the next I'm sliding out, stomach lurching and head spinning. The pleasure is so intense my vision blurs. Suddenly, I'm unable to see, to focus on anything but the bliss spreading from my balls to every inch of my body, spiraling on and on, pulsing through my every cell as my cock jerks inside Emma.

By the time the pleasure is nearly finished with me, she's coming a third time, crying out, "The best ever! The best in the entire world," and I know we won't be sleeping much tonight.

As soon as we've caught our breath, she looks up at me and says, "More, please?" with a smile that is such a perfect mixture of naughty and sweet I can't help but laugh.

And then I give the lady more.

And more.

Until I've lost track of how many times we've both come. All I know is that as we drift off to sleep deep in the heart of that night, heavy in each other's arms, I'm happier than I've been in a long, long time.

I may be sorry later—I know that—but right now, I can't bring myself to regret one second of this absolutely perfect night.

CHAPTER 10

It was a dream. It was all just a dream.

My subconscious stubbornly repeats the mantra as my conscious mind drifts toward wakefulness and I become aware of the slight ache between my legs and the feather softness of my flannel sheets on my bare skin. I'm sleeping naked—I *never* sleep naked; I was raised Catholic for God's sake—and my body is tender in places that haven't been tender in far too long.

And then a warm, heavy arm slides around my waist, pulling me back against Dylan Hunter's also very *naked* body, and any doubt that last night was real vanishes in a rush of breath and body-wide tingles.

"I've got to go soon, Blondie," he says, his erection pressing against my bottom, awakening the hunger I was sure we'd sated last night. "Morning chores aren't going to do themselves."

"No, they won't." My fingers skim back and forth over his lightly furred forearm as I add, in a sex-kitten voice I barely recognize, "But then, neither will I."

He laughs and hugs me closer, his breath warm on the back of my neck. "You're insatiable, woman."

"I'm just committed to the cause." I arch my spine, rubbing my tailbone against his thickness. "I'm only able to conceive today and maybe tomorrow. I haven't been taking my basal temp so I can't be sure, but…" My words trail off as his other hand finds my breast, cupping me beneath the covers as his thumb brushes lazily back and forth across my nipple.

He hums softly. "I see. So the fact that my cock is the best cock in the entire world has nothing to do with it?"

"Maybe a little." My breath catches as he pinches my nipple, sending a surge of electricity straight between my legs. "Maybe a lot."

"I bet you're wet already, aren't you, princess?" His voice is as rough as the palm he skims down my quivering stomach. "Fuck, I love that. How hot you get for me."

"Yes." I nod, not knowing exactly what I'm agreeing to until Dylan urges my leg up and over his, making room for him to enter me from behind.

But oh yeah, *yes* to this. Yes, yes to this a thousand times.

I cry out as the thick head of him presses through where I'm still sore from last night, but the pain is almost immediately banished by a wave of pleasure as he glides deeper, stretching my inner walls, filling me so perfectly I can't believe I ever thought I'd had quality sex before him.

Yes, I've gotten off, but I've never felt anything like the full-body glow that takes over my being as we begin to move together, slow and easy this time, him stroking in and out with deep, sensual thrusts that make me certain he's a wonderful dancer.

He's just...brilliant. The way he moves. The way he holds me so tight, making me feel so precious and safe. The way he kisses my shoulder, whispering encouragement, telling me how amazing I feel, how much he loves being inside me, how hard I make him, how much he wants me to come with him.

To come now...

Now...

"Oh, please, now," he groans, fingers gliding over my clit as we move faster, faster. "Come with me, Emma."

And I do, my body contracting in fierce, beautiful waves that make me feel like I've swallowed starlight, making me glow as bright as the moon outside my window.

The moon that is still bright in the dawn sky when Dylan leans down to kiss me goodbye.

"See you tonight?" he asks. "Around six?"

I nod. "Yes, six is good. But I'll need to pop into the lab before bed and do a last brix check on the juice we brought in last night."

"I can help you with that. I know my way around a refractometer." He pauses, crouching down to bring his face level with mine. "Speaking of knowing my way around... I was thinking about what you said. About you only being able to conceive a couple days a month."

I nod, nibbling my lip to keep from telling some falsehood about weird windows of fertility in order to keep him in my bed on a more regular basis. We have a deal, and sleeping together simply for fun isn't a part of it.

Though, God, I wish it were. I had no idea sex could be this good.

"Well, the way I see it…" He trails off, glancing down at the rumpled quilt, his hair falling into his eyes, making them even harder to see in the near darkness. "Maybe we shouldn't limit this to a couple times a month. I mean, I would think the more I know my way around, the better the chances of success."

"Know your way around…me?"

He looks up, a guilty grin curving his lips. "Yeah. Am I pushing my luck?"

I smile so widely my jaw starts to ache, and hundreds of tiny fireworks explode in my chest. "No, I think you're right. Back when Jeremy and I were trying, my girlfriends were always saying I needed to take things less seriously. Being comfortable and relaxed with your partner is important."

"So, is that how I make you feel, Blondie? Relaxed?" His fingers twine through mine as he presses my hand into the mattress, reminding me of the way he held me down as he took me for the fourth or fifth time last night.

My breath rushes out. "No, you don't make me relaxed. You make me hungry. And wild. Maybe a little crazy."

"Me, too." He kisses my forehead before continuing in a husky voice, "I can't wait to drive you wild again tonight. And don't worry about dinner. It's my turn to cook at the house, so I'll bring leftovers with me."

"Okay," I say, his words making me feel strangely shy. Fucking me is one thing; feeding me is something else. Something that makes me feel cared for in a way no one has cared in a long time.

And though I know it's dangerous to appreciate him too much, I can't help but whisper, "Thank you. For being so sweet."

He grunts. "I'm not sweet. I'm grouchy, and I'm about to prove it by kicking my nephews out of bed and making them help with chores because I'm beat from staying up late banging this smoking hot woman who can't get enough of my cock."

"Well, I heard it was the best cock," I say seriously. "How was she supposed to control herself, I ask?"

His laughter warms me nearly as much as the final kiss he presses to my lips before heading out the door. When he's gone, the room immediately feels colder, but it's nothing I can't handle. Because he's going to be back tonight. And we're going to get to do this all over again.

And maybe by this time next month...

I close my eyes and lay a hand over my belly. I swear it feels different. *I* feel different. And maybe, just maybe...

"Maybe baby," I murmur as my eyes close and I stretch like a cat who lapped up every bit of cream and lived happily ever after with a litter of gorgeous kittens.

CHAPTER 11

DYLAN

One week later...

It is a truth, universally acknowledged, that when the pumpkins get ripe they all get ripe at once and must be picked *immediately*. At least, it's a truth universally acknowledged if you're a pumpkin farmer or have lived next door to a pumpkin farmer for most of your life.

When I see Mr. Stroker toddling up the hill in his starched khaki overalls, swiping a bandana across his forehead in the early morning heat of our third Indian Summer day in a row, I know what's coming.

So do the twins.

Blake pumps his fist in the air, biting off another giant hunk of the turkey sub he made for lunch. "Yes! Pumpkin tossing time. I'm going to kick your ass so hard this year Jacob. I'm tossing two hundred. At least."

"Oh no, not today!" Jacob shakes his head, as if he can banish the old man if he rocks his head back and forth enough. "Raney and I were going to the fair. I already have tickets."

"Looks like it's time to call Raney and make your apologies." I do my best to keep the disappointment from my own voice. It's Sunday, my one day off, and a certain dirty librarian and I had plans to take a picnic, some books, and no clothes down to my secret swimming hole.

I want to see Emma naked and jumping off my makeshift diving board into the river more than I want oxygen, but when duty calls, it calls.

I shoot off a text to Emma, knowing better than to let the twins overhear me talking to a girl. They pretend not to care about "the old folks' love lives" but they haven't stopped giving Rafe shit since he made it his mission in life to make a mockery of Chastity Sutter's first name.

DYLAN: Sorry, I won't be able to take you swimming this afternoon, after all. It's harvest time for the pumpkin patch. Mr. Stroker's on his way up the hill right now.

EMMA: Bummer, but I understand. You're sweet to help him every year. He told me you won't even let him pay you.

· · ·

DYLAN: Lies. The twins and I take home as many pumpkins as we can carry.

EMMA: LOL. So, what's that? Three pumpkins in exchange for a day of back-breaking work?

DYLAN: Don't insult our manliness. We can carry at least two pumpkins each. Jacob has monkey arms, so sometimes he can manage three.

EMMA: Oh, well, I stand corrected. ;)
Still. You're all sweet, and I won't believe any different. Be sure to pack water bottles for everyone. It's going to be another hot one.

DYLAN: I heard. Will do. You stay cool, too, princess, and don't read any naughty books in the nude without me. Especially not with your glasses on.

EMMA: I'll try, but you know how wild we librarians get on our days off...

I LAUGH, and Jacob is immediately there, peering over my shoulder. I hit the home button on my phone and slip it into the pocket of my jeans fast, but not too fast, hoping to avoid arousing suspicion.

"Who was that?" he asks. "Uncle Rafe? The asshole who was smart enough not to come home last night?"

"Don't call your uncle an asshole," I say by way of answer, jabbing a thumb toward the door. "I'm heading out so Mr. Stroker doesn't have to walk all the way up the hill. Get your brother and meet us in the patch in fifteen. And bring the water cooler and cups. We're going to need 'em."

And we do. Holy shit, we do.

By midmorning, we're swiping sweat out of our eyes every few minutes. By noon, we've shed our shirts and are tossing pumpkins half naked, causing more than a few collisions on the bike trail as teenage girls get too busy gaping at the twins to keep their eyes on the road.

The third time I see a girl go head over handlebars, I can't help but laugh.

"I hope you two are behaving yourselves with the girls at school." I cast a meaningful glance first at Jacob, who's taking a water break from cutting pumpkins, and then at Blake, who has put the tractor in neutral while he devours an apple like a starving man.

We have our system down to a science by now, smoothly moving through the rotation of pumpkin cutter, flatbed-surfing pumpkin catcher, and tractor driver in fifteen minute intervals to keep any one of us from getting too miserably sore from the grunt work of cutting and tossing.

"I am," Blake says, mouth full of apple. "But Jacob's a total whore."

"I am not." Jacob flips his brother the bird as he laughs. "You are so full of shit. I've been with Raney since winter break last year."

"Really?" I ask, surprised. "Why didn't I hear a word about her until a couple of months ago?"

Jacob shrugs, squinting out across the field toward the trail. "I don't know. Wanted to keep it quiet I guess."

"In case she dumped his ass," Blake pipes up.

"Fuck you," Jacob says, good naturedly. "I like privacy sometimes, dickhead." He shrugs as he turns back to me. "And it's different with her. It's nice when we keep things just between the two of us."

"I get it." I smile, amazed the pint-size squirt who used to beg me to give him piggyback rides through the barn is becoming such a man. "That's how it should be. When it's right. And real."

"Yeah." Jacob takes a breath, grinning as he swipes his arm across his sweat-soaked forehead. "It's totally like that."

I'm thinking how much I'm enjoying keeping things "just between us" with Emma—we're not teenagers in puppy love, but a simple, straightforward, friends-who-fuck relationship is about as good as it gets as far as I'm concerned—when a girl in a red sundress and a big straw hat waves from the bike trail.

At first I think it's one of the boys' many admirers, but then I catch a glimpse of shoulder-length blond curls and the signature sway of her hips.

Damn, but that woman knows how to move her hips. Memories of the past seven nights at Emma's place and all the incredible things her hips have done to my body threaten to give me a pumpkin-patch-inappropriate hard-on, but I fight it off with a long, cold drink of water.

"Who's that?" Blake asks as Emma starts across the field, toting a jug in her arms.

"Our new neighbor," I say. "The one who bought the Parker place."

"*That's* her?" Jacob grunts in apparent surprise. "I haven't seen her up close yet. Dude, she doesn't look old enough to own a winery."

"Must be rich," Blake observes. "Wonder how she made her money? Whatever it is, that's what I want to major in in college."

"There are more important things than money," I say. "You should pick a career you love. Something you'll get excited about waking up to do every day."

"Screw the money," Blake says in a softer voice as Emma draws closer. "I just want to work with girls who look like that."

Jacob laughs, and I shush them both, warning them to be on their best behavior as I jump down from the flatbed and hurry to meet her, not wanting her to get too close to the twins. They're usually fairly oblivious, but I'm afraid I'll do something to give our secret away. I don't mind people in town thinking Emma and I are an item, but family is a different story.

"Hey, you." She stops beside a monster pumpkin we decided to leave on the ground and roll home in a wheelbarrow later, peering up at me with a grin. "Looks like you guys are tearing through it."

I smile, making sure to keep my back to the boys.

"We're doing our best. Hoping to have some time to play at the end of the afternoon."

"Play time sounds nice," she says, the husky note in her voice going straight to my dick. This woman does things to me, sexy, wild things I wouldn't be at all interested in resisting if there weren't witnesses present.

"I brought you some lemonade," she continues, holding up the lightly sweating brown jug. "Homemade with fresh lemons from my tree."

I reach for the jug, touched. "Thank you. That's thoughtful."

She wrinkles her nose. "Nah, I just don't want you to pass out from heat stroke before I've had my way with you."

"Oh yeah?" I fight the urge to wrap my arm around her waist and pull her curvy body close. Not only are the twins watching, but I also happen to be repulsively sweaty. "So you have ulterior motives?"

"Yes, I do." She glances over my shoulder. "You going to introduce me to your nephews?"

"They're hellions, but sure, come on over." I nod before turning back to the boys. "We've got Jacob on pumpkin-cutting duty and Blake taking point on tractor. Boys, this is Emma Haverford. She brought us some lemonade."

Blake is off the tractor in a hot second, beating Jacob to the jug, though his brother isn't far behind him with our cups.

"Thanks, Miss Haverford," Jacob says. "I was dying for something other than water."

"Yeah, thanks," Blake agrees. "Uncle Dylan only lets us bring water."

She grins, clearly charmed. "You're both so welcome."

"I'm just trying to keep the sugar intake respectable around here," I say, defending myself. "The way your dad told me to."

"I only used a little sugar. And please, both of you, call me Emma." She glances around, lifting a hand to shade her eyes. "Is Mr. Stroker around? I wanted to say hello before I headed for home."

"Nah, Uncle Dylan sent him home," Blake says, pouring his second glass of lemonade. "He's a worrywart."

"It was too hot," I say. "Older people struggle more with heat than we do. We'll save the last row and ask him to come out and help at the end of the day when it's starting to cool down. That way he can be a part of things without hurting himself."

Emma's expression softens. "Sounds wise."

Jacob nods. "Uncle Dylan's the smartest person I know. Even though he didn't go to college like Uncle Tristan."

"And he's funny," Blake adds, stepping closer as he lifts his third glass of lemonade. "When we were kids, he used to do this Elmo impression that slayed. Absolutely slayed. Hard."

"Elmo, huh?" Emma asks, clearly fighting a smile.

"And he dresses up on Halloween and runs with us in the mud run every year," Blake continues. "Not like our dad who is a total fun-killer."

"That's enough, boys," I say, catching on to their not so subtle attempts at matchmaking.

"And he's not bad to look at." Jacob jabs a thumb toward my bare chest. "If you don't mind a little age on the model, that is."

"Stop it. Now," I say, rolling my eyes as Emma hides her grin behind her hand. "Age on the model, my ass. Quit trying to set me up and get back to work."

"But you're a catch, Uncle Dill." Jacob laughs as I lunge for him and just barely miss. He backs away, arms held up at his sides and a shit-eating grin on his face. "It's okay, old man, I can slow down if you're having trouble keeping up."

I point a warning finger at Jacob and then one at his brother, who is yucking it up beside him. "Keep it up, and we can start doing five-thirty get-the-eggs wake-up call instead of six."

Blake presses a hand dramatically to his chest. "That's cruel and unusual punishment. We're growing boys. We need sleep."

"I've read that teenagers really do need more sleep than adults," Emma says, coming to their defense because she's a sweetheart and has no idea that beneath their boyish grins and good manners, these two are Trouble with a capital T.

"See? Emma gets it," Blake says, batting his long lashes in her direction. "Thanks, Emma."

"Five minutes," I warn, eyes narrowing. "And then it's back to work."

The boys retreat to the shade of the tractor, laughing and muttering to each other in their secret twin language, as I turn back to Emma. "Sorry about that."

"Why on earth would you be sorry? They're adorable."

I snort. "Wait until you get to know them better."

"I hope to get the chance." She pauses, brow furrowing as she seems to think better of the words. "Well, I guess I... Considering the terms of our arrangement, I'm not sure if I'll..."

A sharp yelp of distress sounds from the edge of the field, mercifully interrupting the conversation before I'm forced to come up with an appropriate response.

CHAPTER 12

*E*mma spins to look over her shoulder. I lift a hand, shielding my eyes as I squint toward the bike trail. The yelping has been overshadowed by loud cursing as a man in skin tight biking clothes picks himself up from the dirt next to his overturned bicycle.

Just a few feet away, Mrs. Mumford's bulldog, Cupcake, is cowering in the ditch beside the trail, her tail tucked hard between her legs.

Emma and I start across the field at a jog that turns into a run as the thrown biker takes a menacing step toward the dog.

"Hey, what's going on?" I insert myself between the douchebag and Cupcake. "Everything okay over here?"

"Your dog ran into my bike," he spits, jabbing a shaking finger at Cupcake. "Ran right into my front wheel, sent me flying over the fucking handlebars."

"Cupcake isn't my dog, but I'm sorry about that. Are you okay?" I reach for my cell and tug it out of my jeans pocket. "You need me to call for an ambulance? Or help you carry your bike somewhere?"

"No, I don't need an ambulance." His face goes red, emphasizing the light gray stubble on his chin. "I need to be able to use the trail without someone's dumb mutt doing thousands of dollars of damage to my property."

"At least you're not hurt," Emma pipes up from behind me, where she's crouched beside Cupcake, running a gentle hand over the whimpering dog's back. "Cupcake can't say the same. I think her paw is pretty messed up, Dylan. There's some blood, but she nipped at me when I tried to get a better look."

"You should put the damned dog down," Douchebag shouts.

I see crimson, but before I can tell him to shove his fancy bike up his ass, Emma, in a don't-fuck-with-me voice I've never heard from her before, says, "If you hadn't been going too fast, then you would have been able to stop before you hit the dog. The speed limit on this trail is fifteen miles per hour, and I'm sure you were going at least thirty. All the street bikers do."

The man's face flushes a deeper red, but before he can say something he'll regret—I will ensure he regrets it if he turns his temper on Emma—she pushes on.

"And the fact that you have more concern for your property than you do the welfare of another living creature is telling. If you were thinking clearly, I'm sure you wouldn't like the story it tells." She points a finger down the trail toward town. "So I suggest you take your bike, go on your way, and spend some time reflecting on your priorities."

Biker douche's upper lip curls. "And I suggest you shut your mouth, bitch."

I turn back to him, squaring my shoulders and leveling him with a glare that immediately has him taking a step back. "Leave. Now."

"You depend on tourism," he says, his voice edging higher as he scuttles toward his bike. "You rednecks would all be on welfare if it wasn't for our money. You should be kissing my ass."

I take a step forward—one step—but that's all it takes to send the spineless piece of shit scrambling onto his bike. He weaves unsteadily for a few moments—too busy looking over his shoulder to make sure I'm not coming to deliver the ass-beating he so richly deserves —before finding his balance and taking off toward town. Fast.

"Fifteen miles per hour, jerk!" Emma shouts after him. "Slow down! What if you hit a kid next time?"

But the man doesn't slow down, of course. Because some people are determined to be assholes, no matter how many opportunities you give them to behave themselves.

As soon as he rounds the corner, I join Emma at Cupcake's side, holding out a hand, which the dog begins to lick like her life depends on it.

"Hey, there baby, how are you?" I bring my other hand to her scruff, gently scratching the wrinkles around her neck the way she likes while I study her front paw. "Looks like your leg got tangled up pretty good."

Emma hums in concern. "It does. I'm no doctor,

obviously, but I'd bet at least one of her toes is broken. She needs to go to the vet."

"The sooner the better," I agree, meeting Emma's gaze over the trembling dog and nodding to my left. "Mrs. Mumford lives in the subdivision on the other side of that patch of woods. It's the pink house on the right with the gnomes in the front yard, you can't miss it."

Emma stands, dusting her hands off on her dress. "You want me to go get her?"

"If you could just run and tell her I'm on my way with Cupcake. I've known this little girl since she was a puppy. Hopefully, I can convince her to let me pick her up now that the dickwad is gone."

"Got it." Emma nods, glancing both ways before she starts across the trail.

After a little more sweet-talking and scruff scratching, I slide my arm under Cupcake's belly, cradling her ribs in my hand. Being careful to disturb her wounded paw as little as possible, I pick her up, holding her close as I head for Mrs. Mumford's house. The pup whimpers, but she doesn't snap or try to squirm free, and we make it down the narrow path leading to the subdivision without incident.

We've just stepped onto the pavement at the end of the cul-de-sac when Mrs. Mumford appears on her front porch toting a pink pet carrier. Emma is close behind her, holding an oversize purse and a box of dog treats.

"Oh my goodness, thank you, Dylan! You're a gem, as usual." Mrs. Mumford, still looking the way she did when I was ten years old and sat in the third row of her fifth-grade class—steel-wool-colored hair fuzzing around her face and all—hurries down the steps. "How is my baby?"

"I think she'll be fine," I assure her as Cupcake pants faster in my arms, clearly excited to see her human—and treats—headed her way. "Just needs to get her paw checked out, and probably take it easy for a week or so."

"I can't believe she got out of the backyard again," Mrs. Mumford tuts, setting the carrier down by her Subaru and reaching out to cradle Cupcake's face in both hands. "We're going to have to get that fence fixed, aren't we, baby? Poor thing. Here, let's get you a treat to make you feel better."

As soon as the word "treat" is out of Mrs. Mumford's mouth, Cupcake's trembling stops and her tail begins to wag. At Mrs. Mumford's direction, Emma places two treats at the back of the carrier, and I set the dog gently inside. A few minutes later, we have Cupcake loaded into Mrs. Mumford's car and both of them on their way to The Village Vet.

When they're gone, I turn to Emma and smile. "Thanks for helping."

"Of course." She lifts a hand to her hat as a gust of cooler air rushes down the street, promising a break in the heat wave. "It was good to see her excited about the treats. I was worried. She seemed like such a sweet dog, I knew she wouldn't have tried to bite me if she weren't in serious pain."

"Are you okay? She didn't get you, did she?" I take

111

Emma's free hand in mine, turning it over to check both sides.

"No, I'm fine. I have quick reflexes."

I release her slim fingers with a squeeze. "Good. Sorry I didn't ask before."

She smiles. "You were kind of busy scaring away bad guys and saving the day. That was very educational, by the way. If I hadn't seen it with my own eyes, I wouldn't have believed you were capable of looking that scary."

"Oh well…" I cross my arms over my bare chest, cooling down fast now that I'm not slaving away in the hot sun. "The twins taught me a long time ago that a scary look goes a long way. If you get the look down, most of the time you don't have to follow it up with anything else." I sigh. "Speaking of the twins, I should get back. They're good kids, but they're not going to take it upon themselves to start work unless I'm there to remind them we've got shit to do."

Emma glances up at me, studying my face as we turn toward the woods. "You're like a second father to them, aren't you?"

"Hardly." I snort. "I was fourteen when they were born. I'm like a much older brother, I guess. Kind of like my brother Deacon was for Rafe, Tristan, and me."

"Fourteen," she says, surprise in her tone. "So that means you're…thirty-one?"

"I am," I confirm.

She blinks. "Wow. How did I not know that?"

I flash her a grin. "I think you may have been distracted by something more exciting than small talk. At least I hope so."

"Definitely more exciting than small talk. But still, I've never dated—" She breaks off, motioning toward me. "Or, you know, whatever, with someone younger than I am."

"Whatever?" I tease. "Is that what they're calling it these days?"

"You know what I mean," she says, rolling her eyes as we stop to check the trail for speeding bikes before crossing to the other side. "I'm almost thirty-five."

I gasp in exaggerated surprise, pausing at the edge of the patch. "No way. So, does that mean you're a cougar and I'm your prey?"

"Oh, stop," she says, slapping my arm.

"I've always wanted to be cougar bait," I continue, enjoying the blush spreading across her cheeks too much to stop. "To be lured in by an older woman and taught her sexy older lady secrets."

Emma glares. "Not funny, Hunter. Not even a little funny. This is not the way to earn that bottle of Sauvignon Blanc I was going to have chilling for you as a reward for a long day spent helping your neighbor."

"How about I bring over a six pack after I've showered instead?" I let my fingers skim the brim of her hat because I need to touch her and all her other parts are off-limits until I'm clean and away from prying eyes. "We can have beer and burgers?"

"Assuming you can figure out how to work my grill, that sounds wonderful," she stays, still glaring. "So you're not bothered by the age difference at all?"

"No, I'm not bothered. Why should I be? Four years is nothing." I nod soberly before I add, "And from what I can tell, I'm still the senior officer in this arrangement, so…"

"Is that right?" She props a hand on her hip.

"It is. Unless you were lying last night when you said no one had ever slipped his thumb up your ass while he made you come before."

Her cheeks go instantly, powerfully red, and I can't help but burst out laughing.

"Now you're *laughing* at me?" She huffs, but I can tell she isn't angry. "Great."

"I'm laughing *with* you," I correct, still losing it. "You're cute when you blush like a cherry. Or a tomato."

She grabs the brim of her hat, tugging it down until it covers her face.

"No, don't hide. Don't hide, I'm sorry." I bend to catch her eye as I add in a softer voice, "Seriously, Blondie. I'm happy to be the senior officer. I like teaching you new things. Especially things that make you feel good."

"Well, I might have a few tricks up my sleeve, too." She lets her brim flop up as she lifts her chin. "And maybe I'll show them to you tonight. If you're good."

"Oh, I'll be good," I promise, not making any effort to keep the innuendo from my tone. "I'll be very good, princess."

And I am.

And so is she.

Damn, so is she.

By the time she's done this thing to me—a thing that involves my balls in her mouth and her hands everywhere and my brain leaking out of my ears as she makes me come so hard her bedroom ceiling becomes a sky full of stars—I am willing to admit I may have been too quick to claim seniority.

"Mea culpa," I breathe, fighting to get my lungs back under control as she crawls up the mattress to curl beside me. "I was wrong. You were right."

She reaches out, petting the hair on my chest. "Good boy. Good cougar bait."

I laugh. "I wouldn't go that far."

"Oh, I would," she says breezily. "That's your name from now on. I shall call you Cougar Bait and Cougar Bait shall be your name."

"No way, Blondie." I roll on top of her, pinning her wrists to the pillow above her head as her pink lips spread in a satisfied grin. "If you start screaming 'oh, yes, Cougar Bait' when you come for me, I'm going to have to spank you."

Her lids droop and her smile widens. "Oh no, not that… Anything but that…"

I shake my head, trying to pretend I'm horrified but failing miserably. Because I'm already imagining how hot it's going to be to spank her sweet ass while I take her from behind with my hand fisted in her hair.

"Bad girl," I murmur as my cock stirs, insisting he's ready for round two.

"Bad cougar," she corrects, wrapping her legs around my hips. "Admit that I won, and I'll let you be Dylan again. At least until I think of a better nickname."

I rock against her, letting her feel what she does to me, the way she gets me hard mere minutes after I've come like a train barreling off the tracks. "Not so fast. I haven't had my turn. I've got a few tricks left up my sleeve, too."

Her breath catches, becoming a moan as I grind my rapidly swelling length against her clit. "I don't believe you. You're stalling, cougar bait."

"Hang on, princess," I murmur, lowering my lips to hers. "I'm about to prove you wrong."

We don't run out of steam until after two in the morning, at which time we both decide to call this battle a draw—for now.

"To be continued," she sighs, snuggling into the small spoon position where she fits oh-so-perfectly.

"TBC," I agree, relaxing into the feather softness of her bed, the warmth of her body, and the sweet smell of her shampoo, clean linen, and sex.

And it is good. So good, I can't help sleeping over another night.

I'll sleep in my own bed tomorrow. My bed isn't going anywhere, but my nights with this woman are numbered.

Maybe only a couple weeks left. Maybe less, my inner voice supplies as I drift into the haze of half-sleep. *Should know soon if she's pregnant...*

Soon. But not too soon.

There's still time to enjoy each other. Still plenty of time, I assure myself, ignoring the other voice in my head, the one insisting that this is the kind of thing that shouldn't have an expiration date. This is the kind of thing you hold on to so tight not even a starving cougar can rip it from your hands.

CHAPTER 13

EMMA

Six days later...

I love teaching kids new things. And I love coding.

I'm not a corporate slave to a multibillion-dollar tech company anymore, but that doesn't mean I don't still relish the rush of writing an elegant, streamlined piece of magic. Coding can feel like sorcery, sometimes, like I'm a wizard-architect, crafting my own virtual universe.

It's empowering as hell, and I love seeing that same sense of wonder and accomplishment on the faces of my students.

But today I do not want to teach. I do not want to code. I want to run away with the sexy as sin man standing on my doorstep with trouble flashing in his hazel eyes and a picnic basket tucked under one strong arm.

"Hey," Dylan says, breath rushing out. "I just spent

117

two hours going over the books with my dad, and the second he tried to record an entry in the accounting program, he managed to delete the entire September register. And now it's gone. Ten hours of slave labor down the drain. I'm going to be late getting shit to the accountants anyway, so I've decided to ditch work for the rest of the day and get out of town before I strangle my father. Or the twins, who are in the living room playing some loud video game that makes me feel old. Want to come?"

"I do," I say with a grimace. "But I can't. I have to be at my coding class at the elementary school in fifteen minutes."

"Shit, I forgot that was today." His shoulders slump as his brows peak into a pleading upside-down V. "Are you sure you can't play hooky? I packed a picnic." He lifts the basket lid, granting me a peek at wine, fruit, and half a dozen packages wrapped in brown paper nestled against the red-and-white checkered lining.

Lips turning down hard, I shake my head. "I can't. I don't have a substitute, and the girls are already on their way. But I'm bummed. I haven't been on a picnic in forever, and I love unwrapping mysterious edible things. Food presents are the best." I sag against the doorframe with a whimper. "Ugh, and all I packed for lunch is a tuna salad sandwich and cucumber slices."

Dylan pulls a face. "God. That sounds awful."

"I know." I whimper again, eyes squeezing closed. "And it's not even *good* tuna salad. I didn't have any pickles or egg, so it's basically canned grossness with mustard and mayo swirled on top."

"You poor thing, come here." Dylan sets the basket on the ground and pulls me into his arms, making shushing sounds as he dramatically pets my hair, making me laugh as I snuggle into his gray sweatshirt, inhaling the soap-and-Dylan smell of him.

Damn, how does he always smell *so* good?

"But seriously, I'm sorry." I wrap my arms around his waist, leaning into his warmth, wishing I could stay here all day. "About your spreadsheet and missing the picnic. Can I take a rain check? Maybe we can go tomorrow?"

"I have a better idea." His hand wanders down to pat my ass through my jeans. "Why don't I put this picnic on ice and we can have it for dinner?"

I tip my head back, grinning up at him. "Oh, yes, please. That would be perfect."

Dylan nods, still ass-patting as he adds, "And how about I pick you up at the school when you're done with class and we both ditch for the rest of the day? We can get out of town, get into trouble, have a little adventure before we unwrap the food presents."

"Yes and yes." My smile stretches wider. "You're full of brilliant ideas today."

His brows bob up and down. "It's fondling your ass. Gives me all kinds of great ideas." He squeezes my bottom tight before kissing my forehead and bounding away down the steps. "See you at two?"

"Two," I confirm, spirits lifting as I dash inside to toss my tuna in the trash—no sad sandwiches allowed on adventure day—exchanging it for an apple and a granola bar.

A few minutes later, I'm grabbing my lesson plans and heading out the door. And though I know it's probably not wise to be this excited about spending the afternoon with a guy I'll be cutting ties with before too long, I don't try to tamp down my excitement. I don't believe in throwing cold water on happiness, and spending time with Dylan is too much fun to resist.

The two hours of class are peppered with laughter, conversation, coding triumphs, and some truly delicious homemade tortillas, and when we head out the door at two sharp, Dylan is waiting in the parking lot. He leans against his truck, looking like a fantasy come to life in jeans, boots, and a brown sweater that sets off the golden highlights in his hair.

Grin popping back onto my face, I lift a hand, holding up two fingers to indicate I'll be just another second. As I turn back to the computer room door, struggling with the finicky old lock and slightly bent key, Isabella's big sister, Sonia, asks in a hushed voice, "Who's that Ms. Haverford? By the truck?"

"That's my friend, Dylan." I fight to keep the giddy from my voice and fail miserably.

"Your boyfriend, right? I knew you had a boyfriend! You've been holding out on us." Sonia's dark eyes dance as she bounces lightly up and down on her toes. "Oh my gosh, he's so cute! Are you guys engaged? Do you live together? My cousin Tina just moved in with her boyfriend last week, even though they're not engaged, and my entire family is freaking out."

"We're just friends," I say as I fight to free the key from the lock, not wanting to feed her boy-crazy fever.

Sonia's only fourteen, but she and the other older girls are constantly talking about boys and asking me about boys and expressing profound disappointment that I'm not the font of romantic guidance they were hoping for when they learned their coding teacher was a single lady of a certain age.

"Right," Sonia says with a knowing nod. "Just friends. That's what my Tia Mimi said about her boyfriend. Now she's six months pregnant, and last time I checked, friends don't get friends pregnant."

I clear my throat in an attempt to conceal my laughter—she couldn't have hit my arrangement with Dylan more on the nose if she'd tried—but Sonia's too sharp to miss my slip.

"See!" She pokes a finger into my side with a cry of victory, "I knew it! You're not just friends!"

"Hurry up, Sonia," Isabella calls out the window of their mother's Volvo. "We're going to be late to ballet practice!"

"Have fun on your date with your boyfriend," Sonia teases in sing-song as she hurries across the leaf-strewn grass.

"He's not my boyfriend!" I call after her, but I can't stop smiling.

He's *not* my boyfriend, but I have no doubt that we're going to have fun. I always have fun with Dylan, whether we're hanging out on my back porch having dinner or hiking through the apple orchards or playing Scrabble in my office, seeing how many dirty words we can get onto the board before we're forced to take a break and play naughty librarian.

"Hey there, princess." Dylan's lips curve as he watches me cross the parking lot. "Ready to roll?"

"I was born ready." I drop my bag to the pavement and jog the last few steps, leaping into his arms. He catches me with a laugh that becomes a moan of appreciation as I kiss him hard, telling him how much I missed him without saying a word. It's only been two hours, but lately time has a way of stretching out and taking up way too much space when he's not around.

"Watch out, Blondie," Dylan murmurs, his lips moving against mine. "Or we're going to have to take a detour to your place before we leave so I can get you naked."

"Or we could go parking," I say, fingers threading into his hair. "Pretend we're teenagers."

He hums his approval. "Sexy and smart. And I know just the place." He kisses me again, making my head spin before he sets me back on my feet. "But first, we drive. I thought, since you like food presents so much, I'd give you my grand tour of secret local joints. Show you where I get the good stuff." He points a warning finger my way. "Assuming you promise to keep this knowledge to yourself and help keep the tourists away."

I clasp my hands together in foodie-inspired delight. "Yes! I promise. Cross my heart and hope to die with chocolate cake in my mouth."

He laughs as he hauls open the door to the truck. "Then get in, baby."

I do, crawling up into the passenger seat, trying not to make too much of the fact that "baby" has been creeping into Dylan's speech more often than it used to.

I'm not just princess or blondie, anymore. Sometimes I'm baby, and I can't help but enjoy the sound of that particular word on Dylan's oh-so-kissable lips.

"Where to first?" I ask, buckling up.

"It's a surprise," he says, firing up the truck. "But I'll give you a hint. It'll take us a half an hour to get there, but the chef only about thirty seconds to prep our food."

"A riddle. I'm intrigued." I drum my fingers lightly along my bottom lip as I think. "Is it fruit? Fresh off the tree?"

"Nope." He guides the truck west on River Road, heading toward the coast. "Two more guesses."

I wrinkle my nose. "Um...mushrooms? Lightly sautéed? It is mushroom season."

"Strike two," he says, grinning. "One more wrong guess and I get to have you for dinner. That's the way the riddle worked in *The Hobbit*, right?"

"I believe so, but I didn't agree to any dark bargains." I pause, sliding my hand up his thigh as I add in a naughtier voice, "But if you want to have me for dinner, Mr. Hunter, I have no objections. You've cured me of my aversion to that particular type of fun."

He hums beneath his breath. "My pleasure, princess."

I dig my nails lightly into his leg through his jeans. "I think it's my pleasure, actually, but I appreciate your passion for your work. How did you get so good at it? Is that something they take you behind the gym and teach you in Mercyville?"

"My girlfriend, senior year of high school," he says. "Her mom was a sex therapist."

"No way." I snort. "Really?"

"Really. She had all these wild how-to books and plaster models in her office." He shakes his head, lips curving on one side. "Gretchen wasn't a big fan of homework, but as soon as we found the Kama Sutra and a few kinky books from the seventies, we both became enthusiastic students."

"I bet," I murmur. "Though I would have had no idea what to do with kinky books at that age. I was such a nerd."

"Don't believe it."

"Believe it," I say. "I didn't have my first kiss until I was seventeen, and held onto my V card until I was almost twenty-one."

He shoots a scandalized glance my way. "You're kidding. How is that possible? As hot as you are and as much as you enjoy cock?"

I shrug, embarrassed but knowing better than to try to deny the charge. The past two weeks, I've made it clear that I'm practically a cock addict, at least where Dylan is concerned. "I don't know. I was a shy computer nerd obsessed with getting straight A's so I could get into the best grad school." I stretch out my legs, studying my red tennis shoes as I add, "And my mom and dad didn't end well. At all. Kind of scared me off relationships until I was away from all of that for a few years."

"I hear you," he says with a sigh. "My mom and dad didn't end well, either, and after I came to live with Pop, he and my stepmom, Francesca, fought like cats and dogs for two weeks before she threw every wineglass in the cabinet at him and left for good. Turns out she wasn't real happy to find out about Dad's secret kid."

I wince. "I can imagine. My parents liked to throw things, too. Plates and beer bottles mostly, though. They weren't into wine. We weren't that classy."

"Don't believe that, either." He rests his hand on my knee, giving it a squeeze. "You're one of the classiest people I've ever met. I'm actually a little nervous about taking you to a couple of these places. I'll warn you now —they're not fancy."

"I don't need fancy." I take his hand, threading my fingers through his. "If you like them, I'm sure I will, too. I'm easy."

He tightens his grip on my palm with a grin. "One of the things I love about you."

"Ha, ha, very funny," I say as he laughs, and I roll down my window to let in the breeze and pretend my heart hasn't just done a belly flop onto my stomach. He's teasing, clearly, *obviously*, but those words still sound way sweeter than they should.

So sweet, it takes me several minutes to find my equilibrium.

But Dylan fills the silence with another story about a girlfriend of his dad's who, when she caught him cheating, used to chase him around the house with a hockey stick she stole from Dylan's older brother. By the time we turn left on Highway One, following the ribbon of asphalt along the dramatic, rock-studded shoreline, my heart is back in my chest and I have a pretty good idea where Dylan is taking me.

"Oysters, right?" I cross my fingers. "Please say you're taking me to get oysters."

"Not just any oysters," he says. "Point Reyes oysters so fresh they're still squirming when Bobby pops them open."

I pump my free hand in the air. "I can't wait. I've been dying to get out here for oysters, but it seems like there's always one more thing to do. And then one more and one more and before I know it, it's dark outside."

"That's farm life for you," Dylan says. "Watch out, or one day you'll look up and five years will have rolled by without a day off."

"Well, at least I love the work. It's such a change from my old job. I used to be exhausted by lunchtime, and now it seems like I never run out of energy."

His brow furrows. "Yeah, me either. I've never had another job, so I guess sometimes I take how much I enjoy mine for granted. Sure, there are mornings when I'd rather sleep in, or my family is driving me nuts, but most days I feel pretty damned lucky."

"I think that's rare, sadly. A lot of my friends can barely tolerate their jobs. It makes me sad. Life's too short."

"It is," he agrees. "That's part of the reason I want to launch my brewery as soon as I get the farm paid off. Yes, I like what I do now, but I want to create something of my own. Right now, all I make is raw ingredients for other brewers and eggs for chefs. And honestly, the chickens do most of the work there. I'm not going to lie."

"I hear you." I smile as he glances my way, struck

again by how beautiful he is. And it's not just the sun in his hair or the way his dimples frame that pretty smile. It's the way he is, *who* he is, and I have no doubt he's going to accomplish anything he sets his mind to. "You should go for it."

"Yeah?" he asks, expression sobering. "You don't think it's selfish to leave my family to fend for themselves? At least as far as the daily running of the farm is concerned?"

"Not at all. You deserve a chance to go after your dream." I shrug. "And you've got no choice, really. In my experience with big dreams, either you go after them or they go after you."

He laughs, an amused grunt that makes it clear he gets it. "That's what it feels like lately. Like the fire under my ass is starting to burn."

I squeeze his hand, refusing to attach too much meaning to the fact that we've been holding hands in a very not-just-friends way for the past ten miles. "It felt more like being chewed up for me. Like my dream was eating away at me from the inside, making me weaker and weaker the longer I refused to go after what I needed."

Dylan squints ahead at the road. "I get that, too."

"Might be why you've felt grouchy lately," I suggest gently. "Deferring dreams is grouchy work."

"Oh, I don't know." His sexy smile comes out from behind the clouds. "I haven't been grouchy the past couple of weeks."

I smirk. "Sex is a bandage, not a cure."

"What about really amazing, mind-blowing, reality-altering sex?" He winks as he pulls his hand from mine, pointing toward a tiny wooden building on the edge of a windswept cliff. "There is it. Bobby's Oyster Shack."

"It looks like an outhouse," I say, blushing because sex with him is all those things for me, too. All those things and more.

"It used to be, I think." He pulls off to the side of the gravel road. "Bobby moved it here from his family's farm in Cotati. But it's been here for years. No lingering stink left, I promise."

I grimace. "Ew. Maybe I don't want oysters, after all."

Dylan jumps out and trots around the front of the truck to open my door, letting in a fierce gust of sea air. "Yes, you do want oysters. I promise. This isn't something you want to miss, Blondie."

I hop out, following him around to the left of the shack where the structure blocks the worst of the wind. There, behind a counter cut into the side of structure, sits an old man with a long gray beard and kind brown eyes. The moment he sees Dylan, those eyes light up like someone plugged the old man into a socket.

"Dylan! Been too long, son," Bobby says, reaching out to clasp Dylan's hand as Dylan makes the introductions.

After a few minutes of small talk—in which I learn that Dylan has been an oyster addict since he was a teenager, and that Bobby plays in a band with Dylan's older brother when he's in town—Bobby serves us each six oysters in a paper boat with a side of his homemade hot sauce and we wander to the cliff's edge to take in the view of the ocean churning against the rocks below.

To say it's love at first slurp would not be an overstatement.

"Incredible." I moan, savoring the smoky spice on my tongue. "I can't decide which way I like them best, plain or sauced."

Dylan nods seriously. "Me, either. Maybe we should get six more to share, in the interest of research?"

I grin. "Yes. We should. I think it's our duty, in fact."

We return to the counter, and Bobby serves us up another boat, but pauses to point meaningfully over his shoulder as he hands it over. "Remember, oysters aren't just delicious, they're powerful."

"Oysters Make My Clothes Come Off," I read aloud from the front of the tee shirt hanging on Bobby's wall.

"One of the most ancient aphrodisiacs." Bobby nods sagely. "You two be careful."

"Oh, we will," Dylan says, thinly suppressed laughter in his voice. "No worries."

As we wander away, I turn to him and hiss, "Would have been nice to know about the aphrodisiac thing before I'd eaten half a dozen of them. I already have a problem with keeping my clothes on when you're around."

Dylan chuckles as he slurps another. "Don't worry, Blondie. That's just an old fisherman's story. I've been eating oysters for years. Doesn't affect my level of friskiness one way or another."

I harrumph and pluck another from the boat as Dylan leads the way onto a narrow trail winding through the wind-tossed seagrass. "There's an abandoned lighthouse around the bend," he says, motioning with a half shell. "Up for a walk before we head to our next stop?"

"Absolutely." I scan the cliffs around us, noting how isolated this trail is.

In fact, as soon as we round the first corner and the trail dips down a dozen feet, we're out of Bobby's line of sight, tucked away from the road, and so alone we might as well be the last people left on earth.

The realization leads quickly to a plan and the plan just as quickly to action.

Because that's who I am when I'm with Dylan—a woman of action. I wait until we're halfway across the wooden bridge spanning a marshy section of the trail, and then I pounce like an oyster-fueled cougar in heat.

CHAPTER 14

DYLAN

One second I'm walking along, savoring the oyster-eating-afterglow and the feel of Emma's hand in mine. The next, Emma's shoved me against the railing of the bridge, jumped into my arms—locking her legs firmly around my waist—and kissed me hard enough to make my blood pressure spike with an audible pop.

With a moan, I drop the boat and bring my hands to her hips, fingers digging into her ass as I spin, reversing our positions, setting her on top of the railing so I can devote myself to kissing her even more thoroughly. Our tongues wage sweet war, sparing and stroking as the smoke-and-salt taste of the oysters fades, replaced by the taste of Emma.

Sweet, sexy, insatiable Emma, who is quickly making me wonder if I'm capable of going more than twelve hours without getting the shakes from sex withdrawal. Her body is my drug of choice. I know someday—maybe someday soon—I'm going to regret letting myself get so damned hooked, but right now all I can think about is how incredible it is to be this close to her and on my way to getting even closer.

"I'm so sorry," she says when we part long enough to take a deep breath. "It's the oysters. They overpowered me. I couldn't help myself."

I snort, eyes narrowing as she slides her cool hands up the front of my sweatshirt. "The oysters, huh? My irresistible sex vibe had nothing to do with it?"

She bites her bottom lip as her legs tighten around me, drawing my oyster-shell-hard cock tighter to where he always wants to be—inside her, buried deep. "No, I don't think so," she teases, rocking her hips against me. "I think it was the oysters. And you know what that means?"

"What?" I groan as she leans in, nipping at my earlobe before she whispers—

"My clothes are going to come off. It's happening, Hunter. It can happen here or it can happen in that abandoned lighthouse you were talking about, but I—"

Her words end in a yip of surprise as I turn and jog down the trail with her bouncing in my arms, her legs still wrapped around me.

"Put me down!" She giggles as I run faster, and tightens her grip on my shoulders. "We'll get there sooner if you're not carrying me."

"Negative on that, princess," I say, continuing to make swift work of the rest of the trail. "You're under the influence of oysters, and I can't risk you stripping down in the middle of a nature preserve. You could get arrested or catch a cold, neither of which is happening on my watch."

"I'm not going to strip down, you nut. I was kidding. Now put me down."

She laughs harder as I clutch her closer and announce in my best Captain America voice, "Sorry, ma'am. That's not a risk I can take. Hold on for a few more minutes. We're going to get you the help you need."

"The help I need," she echoes, tears streaming down her cheeks. "Oh my God, stop. Stop making me laugh. My lungs are starting to hurt."

"Take a deep breath and hold it," I urge, making a sharp right toward the cliff's edge and the lighthouse.

"I can't," she gasps. "I can't stop laughing. You're insane. Why do people think you're normal?"

I set her on her feet in front of the lighthouse's padlocked door with a soft curse. "I don't know. Good coping skills, I guess. But we've got bigger problems, my little horn dog. Looks like they decided to lock the doors in the off-season."

She makes a distressed sound that echoes the disappointment keening through me. "No! Why would they do that? Don't they know people need somewhere to bang after they've eaten too many oysters?"

I shake my head, breath rushing out. "Because they're bastards, that's why. Bastards who aren't getting laid, so they want to interfere in the getting laid plans of other people."

"Monsters." Emma leans back against the door, her eyes going wide as it swings open behind her. I lunge

133

forward, grabbing her before she can tumble onto her fine ass. "God, what happened?"

"Someone installed it wrong." I reach out, lifting the padlock and letting it fall. "How dumb do you have to do something like that?"

"Maybe they weren't dumb." Emma's arms go around my neck as her voice drops to a husky whisper. "Maybe they were angels of mercy. Rebels with a cause."

My hand skims up her ribs to cup her breast through her pink sweater. "You may be right. And you're absolutely sexy as fuck."

"Oh yeah?" she asks, eyes glittering. "Prove it."

So I do.

First up against the wall, and then with Emma's hands on the wavy glass of the window overlooking the ocean while I come into her from behind, fighting to hold on for as long as possible. And maybe it's how beautiful she is with the sun in her hair, or maybe it's the magical libido-enhancing power of oysters, but I set a quickie record for most orgasms in a twenty-minute session.

By the time we stagger out of the lighthouse, both of us weak-kneed and spent, Emma's been visited by the orgasm fairy three times and I'm pretty sure I did that thing that only Sting can do, where a guy comes, but doesn't ejaculate, and then comes again with enough force to make every muscle in his abdominal wall hurt.

Seriously, my stomach muscles ache like I just spent a solid half hour on core work at the gym, and all I have to say is—worth it.

Totally worth it.

Sign me up for more of this sweet, sweet pain.

When we get back to the shack, Bobby is busy serving a VW van full of surfer hippies, so Emma and I wave goodbye and load up for our next stop.

"The cheese at this place is great," I say as I steer into Point Reyes proper. "But it's going to be hard to top our first stop. We may have peaked too early."

Emma scoffs and wags a scolding finger my way. "No. The peaking was perfect. And who knows, maybe we'll peak again later. Assuming you feed me cheese and wine and chocolate and other things that make my clothes fall off."

Laughing, I park the truck and reach for her, pulling her into my lap because I can't stand the thought of going inside without first getting another fix of her lips. After I've had a long, deep, devoted taste of gorgeous, feisty blonde, I'm able to work up the strength to leave the truck and go in search of cheese.

At Cowpoke Creamery, Emma and I are treated to three of their staple cheeses and a seasonal specialty that brings the heat, but is absolutely fucking delicious.

"Am I crazy," she asks. "Or would this kick ass with Bobby's oyster sauce and some toasted garlic bread?"

I groan in approval of her brilliance as I chew. "Yes. That. We're doing that. Next week. I'll make the twins take the cooler and go pick up oysters and sauce for dinner. They love Bobby."

"He seems so sweet," Emma says. "He has the kindest eyes."

I nod, watching bliss spread across her features as she savors her last bite of the Devil's Smokestack. "He's one of the nicest people I've ever met. Kind to the core. You've got good instincts, Haverford."

She looks up, expression softening. "Thanks."

I lean closer, brushing her hair over her shoulder, not because it needs to be moved, but because I need an excuse to touch her. "Maybe there's something to the oyster thing, after all?"

She grins. "Could be. But I don't see any abandoned lighthouses around here."

"Nope." I sigh. "Then I guess we should try to cool it down. Ready for dessert?"

Emma glances at her watch. "As long as it's not too big. If I eat much more, I won't be able to inflict the damage I want to inflict on your picnic basket."

"Come on." I tug out my wallet to pay for the cheese we've decided to take with us. "I've seen you eat. For a tiny thing, you can take it down. I believe that you can handle waffle cones at the Salty Goat and still put a hurting on our picnic."

"You should have said it was ice cream," she says, looping her arm through mine as we start toward the door. "There's always room for ice cream."

We step out into the sunny afternoon, where the cool bite of the ocean breeze serves as a reminder of how close we are to autumn fading into winter. In two more months, every leaf will be on the ground, seasonal rains will be soggifying Sonoma County, and if Emma and I haven't made a baby by the end of December, this will be over.

Or she'll be gone.

I turn to her outside the Salty Goat, pulling her into

my arms on instinct, because that's what you do when you don't want to deal with reality. She's like the last few weeks of summer as a kid, when you can feel the nip in the air, but go swimming every day anyway, as if plunging into increasingly freezing water will somehow keep summer around forever.

"What's up?" she asks, hands flush against my chest.

I shake my head. "Nothing. Just hate to see the day going by so fast."

"Me, too." She leans into me with a sigh. "I like adventuring with you."

"I like doing most things with you," I find myself confessing, though I know it's stupid. Emma wants a baby from me, nothing more. She's been pretty clear about that from the beginning. And if she'd changed her mind, I would know that, too.

She's a good communicator, which she proves with her next words. "Me, too. I guess that's why it's been so easy to become friends."

"Yeah," I agree, though the word leaves a sour taste in my mouth not even honey lavender hand-churned goat's milk ice cream can banish.

She *is* my friend, but there are times lately when this doesn't feel friendly.

It feels real. And scary. And...incredible.

Like falling in love, that's what it fucking feels like.

I've only been here once before, when I wasn't much more than a kid, but I remember the electricity and the connection and the way something deep inside starts to ache when your person isn't around. In some ways, this is nothing like what I had with Gretchen—Emma and I are adults and there is none of the awkwardness in the bedroom or the emotional upheaval of having big feelings for the first time—but in other ways, it's exactly the same. I hate leaving her and count the hours until I can be with her again. I think about her all the time and dream about fucking her and can remember in vivid detail every single time I've made her come.

Mental scrapbooking of orgasms is a classic warning sign that love is right around the corner.

I should be keeping my distance from Emma, limiting exposure for the sake of keeping my heart from getting blown to pieces when this ends in one disappointing way or the other. Instead, I bundle her back into my truck and take her for a picnic at my favorite spot in the mountains above Armstrong Woods, the one with the view of the ancient redwoods covering the valley below and golden hills stretching all the way to the horizon.

It's romantic as hell.

Glutton for punishment. I am one.

"You can see San Francisco today," I say when we're finished eating and are snuggled under a sleeping bag in the bed of my truck, staying warm as the sun goes down. I point to the sharp edges barely visible in the distance. "There, where the sky is still pale blue."

"I see it," she says softly. "The city feels like another world out here, though, doesn't it? Or another planet."

"Which planet do you like better, city girl?" I ask, tucking my arm tighter around her shoulders.

"This one," she says without hesitation. "I'm not a city girl anymore."

I shake my head. "No, you're not."

Emma fits in here like she was born and raised on a farm. She belongs in this country, on her land, cruising up and down the trail on her bike with her scarf flying out behind her.

I don't want her to go. But if she's already pregnant, I can't ask her to stay. It would kill me to see her moving on with her life with our baby and know I'm just the friendly neighborhood sperm donor.

Don't think about it. Don't ruin the day.

But my thoughts aren't as cooperative as I would like them to be, and by the time we get back to Emma's place—sliding out of my truck under a sky full of stars —I'm crashing hard. So hard I almost make my excuses and head for home to sleep in my own bed for once, but then Emma takes my hand in the dark. "Bath before bed? With candles and one more glass of wine? And the lavender bubble bath I'm not allowed to tell any of your brothers you like?"

I smile. "You can tell them if you want. My manliness isn't that fragile."

"No, it isn't. Not even a little bit." She draws me up the porch steps and into the house, where we come together like words and music, beautiful and true and better together than they are apart. And for now, it's enough, though I can't help but wish she heard the band playing, too.

CHAPTER 15

FROM THE TEXTS OF DYLAN HUNTER AND RAFE HUNTER

Five days later...

*R*afe: Where are you? The boys woke me up, all freaked the hell out. They started on the eggs and realized none of the other chores were done.

They think you're dead. Are you dead?

DYLAN: Shit. No. Not dead.
Overslept. Be right there.

RAFE: You? Dylan, I-wake-before-the-sun, Hunter overslept?

I'm assuming this is in some way connected to the fact that you've slept in your own bed exactly zero times in the past three weeks? You may have been fooling some of the people around here, but I've seen you on your way up the hill at five in the morning.

DYLAN: Just tell the boys to leave the eggs and do the rest of the chores. I'll be there in time to get the orders ready before the vendors come by, but the animals aren't going to appreciate the change in the feeding routine. And the damned cow is going to be a bitch if she isn't milked soon.

RAFE: Don't worry about it. I already fed the animals and milked the cow, who was as sweet as she could be. I think you're making up those biting stories. Moodonna wouldn't snap at a fly biting her ass.

DYLAN: I'll remind you of that when she bites *your* ass. She's lulling you into a false sense of security. That's her pattern. Lull, wait until your guard is down, then bite the shit out of you.

RAFE: Lies. I don't believe a word of it. The cow and I are tight, and the boys handled the eggs, so you're free to linger in bed.

DYLAN: Oh… Okay.
    Well, thanks, I will. Appreciate it, man.

. . .

RAFE: No problem. Though, I will remind you that this is a bad idea. So if you haven't knocked her up yet, I highly encourage you to slap a condom on. Preferably, right now. Do not pass go, do not slide bare into that sweet neighbor pussy.

DYLAN: I'm not discussing this with you.

And don't talk about her. Any part of her, but especially that part.

RAFE: Touchy, touchy. So it's that good, huh?

DYLAN: I'm not talking about this. I'm serious.

RAFE: So, on a scale from damn good time to a magical sex fairy jumped over the moon and slipped anal beads up your ass while giving you a blowjob, she's full fairy?

DYLAN: Gotta go.

RAFE: Condom. Put one on.

Seriously, you're thinking with your dick, and that never ends well. For anyone. That includes her. There's no way she isn't getting the wrong idea with all the sleeping over and sleeping in and disappearing to her place after dinner every night.

DYLAN: Thank you for taking care of things at home. I'll be there soon.

RAFE: All right. I can take a hint.
    But don't say I didn't warn you…

CHAPTER 16

DYLAN

*R*afe's right.

At least, sort of right. I'm thinking with my heart, not my dick, but of the two, the heart is definitely the more dangerous organ.

If I'm smart, I'll roll out of Emma's bed while she's in the shower, leave a note that I'll touch base with her soon, and head back home, where I will stay until I've gotten my shit together and stopped wanting to carve "Dylan hearts Emma" into every tree trunk between my property and hers.

It was never supposed to go down like this. I wasn't supposed to get addicted to her body or the feel of taking her bare in every possible position. I wasn't supposed to sleep over at her place every night and wake up smiling because she's still wrapped up in my arms the next morning. I wasn't supposed to spend every spare minute making her meals, making her laugh, making a fool of myself because I can't stay away from her.

I wasn't supposed to fall.

But her pussy *is* magical, damn it. And she's so much fun to be with. She made it easy to let down my guard and get way too fucking comfortable.

It's only now, after the wake-up call from Rafe, that I realize I haven't slept over this many nights in a row with a woman in…

"Ever," I confess to the ceiling fan whirring gently overhead because Emma and I both like it cold while we sleep.

The realization is enough to take the edge off the boner I've been sporting since I was so rudely awakened from dreams of eating Emma's pussy like my mission on earth was to pleasure her with my mouth.

That's it. No more burying my head in the sand or between Emma's legs or anywhere else. Time to get some distance and think without Emma close enough to kiss, to touch, to surprise in the shower the way I did yesterday.

Though a few more minutes in her company probably won't hurt…

I've got to shower sooner or later anyway…

Tossing off the covers, I tug on boxer-briefs and head for the bathroom, but I pause at the closed door. It's quiet. No sound of the fan or the shower running or Emma humming to herself as she shaves her legs.

I glance back at the clock on the bedside table.

Fuck, it's almost seven-thirty. She must have already showered and headed out to get shit done. She doesn't have animals that require the five-a.m. wake-up call mine do, but her garden is massive, and tending to it usually takes up most of her morning.

Seeing her straw hat is missing from the hook on the wall, my hopes—and the last of my erection—fall flat. I push into the bathroom with a sigh, intending to grab the world's fastest shower before heading for home, only to freeze, curse, and lift a hand to shield my eyes when I discover Emma.

On the toilet.

"Shit, I'm sorry," I say, laughing uncomfortably as I reverse my steps. "I thought you were already gone."

"It's okay, I was just peeing," she says, her words thick-sounding in a way that makes me concerned. I peek through my fingers, and sure enough, her face is blotchy and her cheeks damp.

I let my hand fall to my side. "What's up? Why the sad face, baby?"

She shakes her head. "Nothing. I'm fine."

I frown, concerned. "You don't look fine. What's wrong? Are you sick? Need me to head into town to get you something? Meds or soup or—"

"Tampons." The word ends in a laugh-sob as she scrubs a hand across her eyes.

Oh fuck.

Her period.

Which means…

"I'm sorry." She sniffs and blinks faster. "I'm being ridiculous, and I have tampons. I just really thought…" The edges of her mouth turn down hard. "I was two days late and so hopeful, but then I came in to pee and…" Her face scrunches again, and I can't help myself.

I have to go to her, even if she is sitting on the damned toilet.

"Hey, hey, don't cry." I crouch beside her, giving her a hug as I smooth a hand over her fuzzy, sleep-mussed hair. "We're only one month in. We've still got time. It's going to happen."

"You really think so?" Her arms go around my shoulders as she tucks her face against my neck. "Honestly?"

"Honestly," I affirm. "Next month, no doubt. You'll take your temperature, like you said, figure out the best day, and we'll bang like our lives depend on it."

She sniffs again. "I feel like we do that already."

I smooth my palm over her back through her flannel pajama top. "Are you kidding me? I've got levels of intensity you haven't even glimpsed yet, Blondie. Don't doubt it. It's all going to be okay."

She pulls away, looking up at me with grateful eyes and a soft smile. "Okay. Thanks for the cheering up."

"Anytime," I say, even as a part of me wonders what the hell I'm saying. What I'm thinking.

Yes, I've been gladly going condom-free for the past few weeks, but I've secretly been hoping we would dodge the baby bullet, not land two tickets on the knocked-up train. I don't want Emma pregnant and leaving town. I want her here, with me.

My mouth goes dry as the words rise in my throat. But do I dare? Do I honestly have the balls to ask her to choose me instead of the baby she wants so desperately? To change lanes this late in the Big Dream game?

Before I can decide what to say, to do, Emma gently

pats my cheek. "But now you have to go," she says. "Because this is embarrassing."

"Are you sure?" I ask, grateful for the excuse to keep things light. "I've never hugged a woman on a toilet. We could make out if you want. Add to the list of firsts."

Her nose wrinkles. "Ew. No. Stop."

"You're sure?" I tease as I back toward the door. "I'm down with fulfilling your toilet fantasies, baby. I'm a gentleman on the street, but I'll be your freak on the can."

Eyes glittering with laughter instead of tears, Emma jabs a finger toward the door. "I have no toilet fantasies, weirdo. Now get out of here!"

I make a break for it, closing the door behind me with a laugh.

But as soon as I'm out of Emma's sight, my smile slips away.

I've always prided myself on telling it like it is—to my brothers, my friends, even my dad—but with Emma... I don't know how to cross this bridge with her, or if she even wants to cross it.

I could call off Operation Baby Bump now—while I know I'm in the clear—and beg her to consider a new arrangement, one where we date for real and just...see where things go.

But even as the thought zips through my head, I know better. I know *her* better than I did before. She's as stubborn as she is sexy, and she will absolutely find another man to fuck a baby into her if I won't.

And I do not like the idea of another man in this bed with Emma, his dick trespassing in my territory.

No…she's not *mine*. Not even close.

That's dangerous thinking, any way you slice it.

I dress quickly, trying to think of some more potty jokes to lob at Emma on my way out, determined to get home and start seeking clarity regarding the mess I've gotten myself into. But when Emma emerges wearing jeans and the weathered blue sweatshirt she prefers for cool mornings, I don't have any jokes. Or clarity.

All I've got is an idea I hope might cheer her up.

"Want to come to the harvest parade with me tonight?" I ask as I shrug on my jacket. "See if the 4H club brings home another winning float this year?"

"I don't know." She leans against the bureau beside the bathroom door. "I thought we were keeping a low profile. You know, so people won't get nosy."

"We'll keep our hands to ourselves while we're in public and go as friends. You're my neighbor. No reason you shouldn't catch a ride into town. Parking's always a pain in the ass, so lots of people carpool."

"Or we could ride bikes," she says, eyes lighting up.

I curl my lip, playing up my disdain. "You and the bicycling everywhere…"

"It's fun," she says, crossing her arms. "And good exercise."

"I get plenty of exercise."

"Yes, you do." Her gaze flicks up and down, making my cock thicken because he is *that* easy around this woman. Just a look, that's all it takes. "But are you getting plenty of fun, Mr. Hunter?"

I sure have been lately. Aloud, I say, "All right, bike it is. I'll text you when I'm on my way over, okay? We should leave around five to get a good spot."

"Okay. Sounds good." She props one foot on top of the other, her toes squirming into the thick carpet.

"You sure?" I eye her feet. "'Cause those tend to get wiggly when you're worried about something."

She laughs guiltily as her toes still. "Your powers of observation are scary sometimes."

I arch a brow, silently encouraging her to spit it out.

"I just…" She flaps a sleeve in my direction. "I'm not going to be very much fun after the parade. I know some people don't mind getting busy while they're surfing the red tsunami, but I'm not one of them."

I huff as I realize what she's saying. "The red tsunami, huh?" I step into my boots, reaching down to tug the loop at the back as I assure her, "It's fine, Blondie. We're capable of enjoying each other's company without getting naked."

"Yes, we are," she says, a grin curving her lips. "Though I will look forward to getting naked with you again on Wednesday."

I do the math—four days, over ninety miserable hours—and fight the urge to beg her to reconsider her stand on this. I'm a grown man, for God's sake. I'm a lot more concerned about not getting into her pants than I am a little mess. This is why our ancestors invented shower sex, after all.

But the four days will probably be good for me, help me recover some of that perspective I've misplaced the past few weeks and decide what to do about that fact

151

that I'm every bit as addicted to Emma's laughter as I am her body.

"Me, too." I reach for the door to her bedroom. "See you tonight, princess. And don't be afraid to give me a call if you need more cheering up."

"Thanks," she says softly. "You're the best, Cougar Bait."

I smile, but I don't respond. I just wave and head for the door because I'm not the best. I'm the worst. I've taken a perfectly good friends-with-benefits situation and fucked it all up. And now, there might be no way back and no way out. It all depends on whether or not I can convince Emma that this thing growing between us is worth putting her dreams on hold.

CHAPTER 17

EMMA

I pass an unexpectedly peaceful morning—considering the less than stellar way it started—grateful for the autumn sun on my face and the view across the vineyard. No matter what disappointments the day holds, there is always this breathtaking view, the dirt—dark, rich, and alive beneath my fingers—and the joyful pulse of this land where I went looking for fulfillment and discovered I already have everything I need to be happy inside my own skin.

All but that one thing...

I turn, glancing up the hill to see Dylan headed toward the barn. The moment I lay eyes on him, my heart lifts. He's too far away for me to see his face, but I would recognize him anywhere—from miles away, from a flash of his smile in the dark, from the touch of his hand when there is no light at all.

He gives off his own light, this man who tries so hard to hide the big heart beating in his perfect chest.

Sometimes I want to ask him what he's afraid of,

what he fears will happen if he drops the tough guy act completely and lets the world see who he really is. See how much he cares about his family and this town and the land that thrives under his care, because even Mother Earth can't help but respond to his touch.

But those are the kinds of questions that lead further down the rabbit hole, and I'm already so far down. So far up. So lost in the way he makes me feel that I'm dangerously close to losing my grip on reality.

Just because a man hugs you on the toilet, doesn't mean he feels the way you feel. You know how he is. He can't stand to see anyone or anything in pain. He would have done anything to make you stop crying.

And just because he brings me dinner and beer and books he thinks I'll like, it doesn't mean I'm in his thoughts as often as he's in mine. And just because we have so much fun together that I've been counting the minutes until our next adventure day, and just because he makes love to me like he'll die if he can't have me again, and just because, because, because...

"Because of the wonderful things he does," I sing softly to myself as I stand with my arms full of freshly harvested kale and head for the kitchen.

He *is* wonderful, but he's also temporary, no matter how much I might want things to be otherwise. I've just got to keep walking the tightrope, finding a way to balance how much I'm coming to care about Dylan with the knowledge that our relationship is a business arrangement with benefits.

But when the knock comes on my door just before

five, I practically dance across the den, feet barely touching the floor I'm so excited to see him again.

But my grin fades as I throw open the door to see not one, but two drop-dead gorgeous Hunter men on my front porch. "Oh, hi."

Dylan jabs a thumb his brother's way. "This is Rafe, which I'm sure you already know, but he said it was time he was properly introduced. Wouldn't take no for an answer. Followed me over here like a total pain in the ass."

"Just like my brother." Rafe grins as he takes my hand. "Nice to meet you, Emma. Dylan isn't much of a talker, so I haven't heard nearly enough about you. So tell me everything. Where are you from and how are you enjoying country life and how can you put up with my brother for such long stretches at a time without strangling the cranky bastard?"

"He's not cranky, he's charming," I say with a laugh, even as I absorb the insight Rafe's provided—more evidence that Dylan and I are just friends who get it on, and I'm certainly not someone he discusses with family members.

Rafe arches a brow. "Charming? This one?"

"I'm only cranky when people are complaining about my cooking," Dylan says, looking uncomfortable. "Or second-guessing every decision I make."

"Dad is the second guesser," Rafe says in a confidential voice. "I'm the one who complains about his cooking. But I'm a fucking rock star in the kitchen, so I may have unreasonable standards."

I laugh again as I grab my coat. "I'm a fan of his

cooking, too. But I'm easy to please when it comes to food. The only thing I can cook without burning it to a crisp is grilled cheese with a tossed salad."

"But you make a mean tossed salad." Dylan reaches out to squeeze my hand, mouthing, "I'm sorry" as Rafe starts down the steps in front of us. I return the squeeze with a smile, silently assuring him that I don't mind his brother tagging along.

This isn't a date, after all. It's two friends hanging out, and Rafe will serve as a great reminder of that.

As I fetch my bike from the barn, I answer Rafe's questions—I'm from San Francisco originally, with a ten-year interlude in Silicon Valley, and I'm loving country living—and on the way into town, he tells me what Dylan was like when he was a kid.

"When he moved in with us, he could already read," Rafe says as we glide along—him on one side of my bike and Dylan on the other. "Five years old and reading at a sixth-grade level or some shit. Dad was so fucking impressed and I was *soooo* pissed. Meant I had to bust my ass to catch up." He laughs, his hundred-watt smile making it hard to imagine him angry. Rafe is intense, no doubt, but he also seems like the kind of person who doesn't worry about the little things, and who considers almost everything a little thing.

"Wow." I cast an impressed look Dylan's way. "Reading like that at five?"

"Not because I was smart," he says, rolling his eyes. "I was just bored. We didn't have a television at my house, or many toys. But the library was five blocks away, and the librarian handed out lollipops and jawbreakers, so..."

"They didn't have power, either," Rafe offers. "Or indoor plumbing. Dylan's from hardcore hippie stock. Showed up on our doorstep with bare feet and hair down to his ass. That's how he got his nickname."

"Don't you dare," Dylan warns, but he's laughing as Rafe says, "Don't be ashamed, Goldilocks. I'm sure Emma's noticed that pretty hair of yours."

I giggle. "Oh man, I wish I could have seen that. I bet you were adorable."

"Don't worry, I've got pictures," Rafe says with a wink. "Come over for dinner tomorrow, and I'll whip out the family albums."

"Emma is not coming over for dinner," Dylan says, humor vanishing from his tone. "I'm not about to subject her to all of you at once. One or two of us at a time is more than most sane people can handle."

I'm tempted to remind him that I'm not the sanest girl around—I *was* having a meltdown on the toilet just this morning, after all—but bite my tongue. He doesn't want me coming over to his place, or he would have invited me himself. Instead, he's been very careful to keep all our interactions confined to my place or on otherwise neutral turf. More evidence that the warm, smooshy feelings I experience when I'm with him are completely one-sided.

So I smile at Rafe and say, "Thanks for the offer, but I already have plans."

"What kind of plans?" Rafe asks, proving he has zero issues with putting people on the spot.

"I'm going to see my sister in Berkeley," I lie, even as I decide to do my best to make the lie a truth. It would be good to see Carrie, to hang out, shop, eat, and forget about babies, bargains, and beautiful men who are too damned irresistible for their own good. In fact, "I'll probably stay the night."

"Oh no." Rafe's features crease with concern. "Are you going to be able to survive that, bro? If Emma is gone for an entire twenty-four hours?"

"Shut up, Rafe," Dylan mutters.

Rafe speeds up, meeting Dylan's gaze over the front wheel of my bike. "I mean, I know I'm not supposed to know that you two are special friends, but the grass is getting pretty thin on the path across the field to her place."

"Seriously, drop it." Dylan's hazel eyes burn as he glares at his brother. "Now."

Rafe lifts both of his hands, balancing with apparent ease with only his feet on the pedals. "All right, all right. My apologies, Emma, if I stepped out of line."

"It's fine," I say, forcing a smile.

But I'm not sure it is…

The conversation returns to more neutral topics—the history of the harvest parade, the best places to watch the festivities, and whether caramel corn or caramel-coated apples are the must-have snack—but I'm only half-listening. I can't stop thinking about unforeseen complications and things Dylan and I might not have thought through when we made this arrangement.

After we've parked our bikes outside Barn Roasters,

I hang back, signaling to Dylan that I'd like to have a word in private.

"We'll catch up with you," Dylan says, waving his brother on. "Save us seats."

Rafe nods and lifts a hand, disappearing into the crowd swarming downtown, where the streets are already closed off for the parade. I lead the way around the side of the old barn and turn back to Dylan with a furrowed brow. "Maybe we should stop this."

He blinks. "Stop what?"

I motion between us. "Me and you. This. Our arrangement. Obviously your brother is getting suspicious."

"You mean Rafe?" Dylan's eyes lift to the evening sky. "He's not suspicious; he's a pain in the ass."

"He's curious about who his brother appears to be dating," I say. "That's not being a pain in the ass. That's normal. But what we're doing isn't normal, and sooner or later the *not normal* is going to come out. I know how hard it is to keep secrets from family, and I wouldn't want to—"

"He knows, Emma," Dylan cuts in, stealing the rest of my words away. "The morning after you made your offer, I talked it over with Rafe and my younger brother, Tristan. I didn't tell them what I decided—I figured once the decision was made it was between you and me —but they know. And Rafe has…opinions about it."

"Oh." I cross my arms and rock back on my heels, not sure whether to feel embarrassed or exposed or something else entirely. "So what are his opinions?"

"He thinks we should stop." Dylan shoves his hands

into the pockets of his jeans, the threadbare pair that make his backside look especially lovely. "Or at least take several steps back. But it's none of his business what we decide to do. I've tried to tell him that, but he thinks he's got to look out for me, even though *I'm* the one who takes care of other people's shit. I'm the one who got him the loan to open his business and who's helping him fill out the insurance claim paperwork and—"

He breaks off with a shake of his head and a tired sigh. "Sorry. I'm rambling. It's not his fault. It's my fault. I shouldn't have let him tag along. I'm sorry. You shouldn't have had to put up with uncomfortable questions on a day like today."

A day like today, when I found out I wasn't pregnant by a man who wants nothing to do with me, or our baby, should I be lucky enough to conceive. A day like today, when I once again completed the mental gymnastics necessary to make it okay to keep falling for Dylan, despite the warning signals flashing bright red every step of the way.

A day like today, when maybe I'm finally ready to listen to the wake-up call Rafe is sounding, loud and clear.

"Maybe he's right," I say, triggering a howl of dismay from my heart, which isn't at all pleased at the thought of taking a step back. It wants to get closer, closer, until there isn't a centimeter of space between Dylan's soul and mine. "Maybe we should take a break."

His brows draw sharply together. "Why? Because my

brother has an opinion? I didn't realize he was a part of this equation."

"Well, he is." I lift my hands at my sides. "I mean, in a way. He would be the baby's uncle. Maybe he doesn't like the idea of having a family member he'll never get to know."

"Yeah, right," Dylan says with a hard huff. "We could have brothers and sisters we'll never know. We both realize that. It's part of being a Hunter. Part of our Dad and every other man in our family sticking his dick where he shouldn't be sticking it and not worrying about the consequences."

"So maybe *we* should be more worried about consequences," I say, my chest starting to ache.

There it is, the truth. He still expects me to disappear if we hit the baby jackpot.

But of course he does. I was a fool to imagine anything had changed.

"Maybe we rushed into this," I continue in a softer voice, "and now we need to hit pause and think things through in light of new information."

"New information like what?" he asks.

New information like the fact that I think about you all the time and I'm pretty sure I'm clinically addicted to your penis.

But I don't have the chance to confess my weakness before Dylan rushes on, "You know, you're probably right. I had doubts about this from the beginning, but there you were in your sexy librarian outfit, practically begging me to knock you up, and I made choices against my better judgment."

I narrow my eyes. "That's not how I remember it. I remember talking things through and coming to a compromise that worked for both of us. That's why I promised to move away if we get pregnant."

"If *you* get pregnant," he snaps. "I'm not part of that, remember?"

I flinch, blinking fast as I take a step back.

Dylan sighs, his crossed arms falling to his sides. "Shit, I'm sorry. I didn't mean that. Not the way it sounded, anyway."

"No," I say softly. "I think you did. And you're right."

"I'm not right. Come on, Emma, let's not do this." He reaches for me, but I step away, and he pauses, frustration creeping into his features. "Please. Everything was good before Rafe stuck his nose into this. Let's hit rewind, forget we fought, and go enjoy the parade."

But I can't forget the fight or all the unpleasant facts Rafe highlighted in bright yellow marker for me. Dylan does not feel the things I feel, not even close, and it would be dangerously stupid to keep skipping through the sex forest with him, ignoring the heartbreak wolf lurking in the shadows, ready to do serious damage to my emotional well-being.

I need to think. To breathe. To decide if making a big dream come true is worth the pain waiting around the corner.

"I should go home." I force the words out through a tight throat. "See you later, okay?"

"Emma, please." Dylan follows me as I circle back around the barn to the bikes. "Don't go. Stay. Let me buy you a caramel apple, and we can make fun of the miniature pony costumes."

"I don't want to make fun of the poor ponies," I mumble, spinning the combination on my bike lock.

"It's okay, the ponies are in on the joke. The guys at the mini pony farm dress them up every year, and they prance up and down Main Street like celebrities. It's a harvest parade tradition." Dylan puts his hands on my handlebars, holding the bike still as I try to pull it free from the stand. "Please. Don't go. Or at least don't go mad. I'm sorry."

"I'm not mad," I say honestly. The ache in my chest intensifies as I meet his gaze, where swirls of green and gold mix in his eyes. Those eyes that make my soul feel like it's being turned inside out when he's moving inside me, looking like he's never seen anything more captivating than me at his mercy.

But of course he has, and it's high time I thought about what it means for me to be so much more attached to him than he is to me.

"I just need some space, some time, okay?" I force a smile, refusing to get weepy in front of him again.

"Emma, please…" Dylan's brow furrows and his eyes fill with regret, but when I tug on the handlebars, he lets go without a fight. He doesn't really want me to stay; he just hates seeing people upset.

I keep my fake smile plastered on my face as I wiggle my fingers. "See you around. Have fun and no worries. Everything's cool."

* * *

BUT EVERYTHING IS *NOT* COOL, a fact that becomes abundantly clear when I wake up the next morning and immediately long to call Dylan with every fiber of my being.

But I can't, and soon a long walk off a short pier starts to sound like a good idea.

When the Doldrums Monster attacks this hard, there's only one course of action to take. I text Carrie, insist on taking her shoe shopping in approximately seventy minutes—sooner if the traffic on the 101 South isn't ghastly—and head for the Audi A5 I hardly drive anymore.

Because some places are too far to reach by bike, and right now I need to be far, far away from the house on the hill and the beautiful man sleeping inside it.

CHAPTER 18

EMMA

$\mathcal{I}$ head to Berkeley, and a Sunday afternoon of sisterly bonding ensues. But not even shopping with Carrie at our favorite shoe store—the one that sells the sky-high heels that make me nearly as tall as a normal person and badass boots that compliment Carrie's uniform of pleather pants and ripped up sweatshirts—can take my mind off my worries.

"Guy trouble?" she asks as I sigh for the fifth time since we sat down to order cupcakes and afternoon coffee. "Sexy Farmer turn out to be an asshole like I thought?"

I shake my head. "No."

I frown. Sigh. Purse my lips.

"It's just..." More sighing. So much sighing. "Complicated."

"Sounds like you've been holding out on me," Carrie says. "Not to say I told you so, but this is what happens when you date a douchebag who acts like he's doing your pussy a favor with his dick. You should have kicked him to the curb before he could get his pants off."

"Stop," I whisper, glancing around the café, grateful to find no one seems to be eavesdropping on our conversation. "I don't talk about sex stuff in public. You know that."

She lifts an unsympathetic brow. "Then you should have called me and confessed instead of showing up for shopping and cupcakes all constipated with secrets."

I huff. "I am not constipated with secrets."

"Talk, woman." Carrie crosses her arms, pinning me with a hard look that makes her heavily made-up blue eyes look even more dangerous. "Spill, before I cut the truth out of you with this butter knife."

"Stop, you're scaring me," I lie. But I know I'm only putting off the inevitable. I always break with Carrie. I'm literally incapable of keeping secrets from my sister.

She shakes her head, sending her bleached white hair with the purple streaks flopping into her eyes. "Seriously, sweet pea, why do you insist on finding the biggest asshole in your immediate vicinity and then jumping onto his cock?"

"That's not what happened," I say, nose wrinkling at the reminder of how many jerks' names I've managed to collect on my dance card. But Dylan isn't a jerk, he truly isn't. And I don't like Carrie having such a low opinion of him, even if they will probably never meet again.

So I tell her the truth, the entire sordid, crazy tale, while she makes a wide variety of snorts, clucks, grunts, and *tsks* that most people would have trouble deciphering. But I've had twenty-nine years to learn my sister's language, and by the time I'm done, I already know exactly what she's thinking.

"See?" I point a finger at her chest. "I wasn't doing my usual asshole thing. I was being smart and logical before I screwed it up by getting attached."

Carrie presses her knuckles to her lips as she thinks. "Okay," she says. "So, this is what I'm hearing…"

I lean in, cupping my steaming coffee mug with both hands, waiting with bated breath because Carrie's insights are almost always excellent.

"I'm hearing that this douchebag is actually…*not* a douchebag."

I nod impatiently. "Yeah, that's what I said. He's nice. Really nice."

"Oh, I didn't say he sounded nice," she corrects as she peels the wrapper from her red velvet cupcake. "Any guy who stays over at your place that many nights in a row isn't being nice, he's clearly got an ugly hard-on for you in the worst way."

"There's nothing ugly about it," I mumble, but only shake my head when Carrie asks me to repeat myself.

She *harrumphs*, eyes narrowing as she surveys me over the mountain of icing she's poised to bite into. "So to me that means one of two things. One, he's actually really into you and probably not just in a physical way because even sex addicts need a break to get some sleep now and then."

My heart lifts, only to tumble down the hope hill as she adds, "Or, two—and more likely, sadly, because people are the worst—he's got intimacy issues. And he's getting codependent with you way too fast because his parents didn't make him feel special and he's got a gaping hole in his heart where the unconditional love was supposed to go."

My lips part in protest, but close before any words come out.

Intimacy issues… I don't think that's the case, but it's weird that Carrie guessed part of Dylan's backstory without me saying a word.

She takes an enormous bite of her cupcake, but I'm still chewing on my thoughts by the time she's finished the bite then taken a sip of her coffee. "He's got issues, right?" she prods.

I shake my head, nibbling at my bottom lip. "I don't think so. He's not needy or anything like that. Most of the time, he's generous in every sense of the word. The kind of person who takes care of the people around him, not vice versa." I hesitate a moment before adding in a halting voice, "But his mom did kind of drop him off at his dad's place when he was five years old and never come back, so…"

Carrie winces in a rare moment of empathy. Not to say my sister doesn't have a heart—she does—she just believes people are made of tougher stuff than the self-help gurus give us credit for. "Yikes. That sucks. Poor kid."

"Yeah," I agree. "But he seems to have come out of it okay. He runs his family's farm, takes care of his big brother's kids while he's deployed, manages all the finances, even some of the stuff for his other brother's motorcycle repair shop if I understand it correctly, and he—"

"Got it, got it." She nods quickly, licking icing off her thumb. "So he's the guy who deals with abandonment by taking care of everyone's shit, being the perfect son-brother-uncle-farmer, and making sure he's so busy being the man in charge that he never has to deal with being out of control."

I hum, lips puckering as things start to sound familiar.

Carrie isn't a therapist—she studies psychological profiles to add depth to the characters in her books—but in the past few years, she's gotten eerily good at predicting real life people's issues. I'm sure the time we both spent in therapy growing up, dealing with the fallout from our parents' miserable breakup, didn't hurt when it came to honing her skills.

"He goes to great lengths to avoid being vulnerable and exposed," Carrie continues, warming to her topic. "Because that would let someone into his feelings cave, and he's shut down the feelings cave because the first woman who ever visited was an asshole who told him his cave was ugly and left without waving goodbye."

"Ugh." My shoulders curl as my stomach starts to hurt, which is a shame because I haven't had a single bite of my Mocha Dust cupcake. "I think that might be it."

"Any serious ex-girlfriends hanging around?" Carrie asks.

I shake my head. "No serious exes since high school. Not that I've heard about, anyway, and people *talk* in that town."

Carrie shudders. "Small towns. So awful. I don't

know why you're subjecting yourself to that of your own free will."

I roll my eyes, refusing to get distracted defending Mercyville. It wouldn't make a difference to a die-hard city lover like my sister, anyway. "It sounds like he's dated casually," I continue, "but ends relationships amicably before things get too intense."

Carrie nods. "Yep. I would bet my right hand that bucko's got abandonment issues. And probably the only reason he let you get as close as he did is because you two agreed up front that feelings weren't going to be part of your arrangement." She wiggles her fingers. "You snuck in there under his radar, all sneaky like."

"But now feelings are involved," I say softly. "At least for me. I really like him. Like…a lot."

Carrie sighs, popping the last bite of her cupcake into her mouth and chewing before she asks, "How much a lot?"

I thread my fingers tight together, squeezing them into a fist in my lap as I confess, "So much that I'm going to give up on trying to get pregnant because I think another month or two of having sex with him would get me so hooked that my heart would be sad, pulpy pain-mush when it was over. And you know how much I want a baby."

She frowns, holding up a hand in the universal sign for "hold up a second." "Why? Why are you doing that to yourself? If you're going to have a broken heart, at least get what you wanted from the arrangement first."

I shake my head. "You don't understand. I can't. It's not going to work anymore."

"Because you're getting out now, before you get hurt?" Carrie arches an eloquent brow that communicates exactly what she thinks of that MO. "Now who's letting her abandonment issues take the wheel?"

"I am not," I protest, swiping a finger through my frosting and popping it into my mouth. "Don't analyze me."

Carrie taps her chin. "There's a song about Jesus taking the wheel, right? But I don't seem to remember a song about abandonment issues taking over. Probably because that would be a shitty idea, even for a country song, and they love to sing about sad, shitty things that make people feel awful."

"I'm starting to like country music, actually. The country station in town is really good. Nice mix of classics and new stuff, not too many drinking songs. I'm not big on drinking songs. Is that weird? Considering how much I enjoy a glass of wine?"

Carrie's eyes go wide, and her lips peel slowly away from her teeth in a horrified grimace, making me laugh.

"Stop it." I kick her boot beneath the table. "You look like you're about to throw up."

"It could happen." She shudders again. "Who are you? And what have you done with my classic rock and Celtic folk song loving sister?"

I shrug. "I'm keeping an open mind. Making room for new experiences, new likes and dislikes, new sides of myself."

Carrie nods, a smile creeping across her face that makes me positive I've stepped into a trap, even before she says, "So that means you *don't* walk away from this thing with Sexy Farmer. That's what old, stuck-in-her-ways Emma would have done. New Emma is going to be brave and see this through until she's knocked up with a beautiful bouncy baby boy."

"Or a girl." My heart beats faster at the thought of a little girl playing in the dirt beside me while I garden, a bundle of energy with Dylan's hazel eyes and dimpled smile.

Though of course, that's part of what makes this so hard...

"Even if I can convince him to pick up where we left off," I begin slowly, only for Carrie to snort and roll her eyes.

"He's hot after your sweet ass. He'll pick up where you left off. Trust me."

"Even if I can convince him," I continue, "and I manage to get pregnant, no matter how far away I move, I'm going to be taking Dylan with me. My son or daughter will be a walking, talking reminder of the man I let myself fall so hard for and all the mistakes I made."

Carrie's expression softens. "Baby girl, every good thing has a poop sandwich."

I wrinkle my nose. "A poop sandwich?"

"Yes, the shitty part of the thing you love. I was listening to *Big Magic* by Elizabeth Gilbert the other day, and it reminded me about the unavoidable shit sandwich. Think about it—your job, your relationships, even your hobbies—there's a down side to everything. I love writing, playing pretend with my characters in my office all day, but I hate marketing like fire ants in my panties. That's my shit sandwich."

I nod, catching her drift. "So my shit sandwich would be waiting for my wine to age so I can see how it's turned out. Growing, tending, harvest, crush—all of that is the fun stuff. But the waiting is a bitch."

"Exactly. But you're willing to wait. You'll eat that shit sandwich and keep on making wine because it's your passion." She pauses, pinning me with a loaded look. "And if I'm not mistaken, becoming a mother—something I know you've dreamt about forever—is going to be worth chomping an even bigger poo biscuit."

I stick out my tongue. "Stop. I get it. No more potty talk."

Carrie leans in, elbows braced on the table, "Okay, but think about it, Em. You'll have a baby to shower with love. Your heart is going to be so full that it will make things like an infant keeping you up all night, or feeling sad that her father isn't in your life, seem small in comparison."

I press my lips together, torn.

"Trust me. It will be worth it," Carrie urges.

I hum thoughtfully as I bite into my cupcake, relishing the bittersweet dark chocolate icing mixing with the coffee flavored cake. Even in this bite, there's bitter mixed in with the sweet, but it highlights the softer flavors, making them shine.

So maybe Carrie's right…

Maybe I can make this work. "Thanks for listening," I say, smiling as my eyes fill with hopeful tears. "You're the best sister ever."

"Any time, sis. But don't cry." Carrie laughs as she

squeezes my hand. "Geez. Are you sure you're not already pregnant?"

"Nope." I motion dryly to my cupcake. "There's a reason I was craving chocolate. Though, it has been super light so far."

She groans. "Lucky you. Mine is a fucking nightmare. I'm so over it. I can't believe I have twenty more years of this to look forward to. Next life I'm coming back as a dude or a tree or some sort of creature that doesn't menstruate."

From there, our talk turns to the usual sisterly topics of the evils of the red tsunami, the reasons Carrie should move out of her studio above the toy store she still manages, despite the growing success of her books, why Dad is trying to raise goats when he knows nothing about goats and is bad at keeping things alive, when Mom is coming back from her latest singles cruise to Alaska, and whether *Dancing with the Stars* will ever consider writers "stars" so Carrie can audition.

"Maybe if I can sell half a million copies of the next book?" she asks, stopping to pet a bulldog wearing a pink studded collar as we make our way through downtown Berkeley.

"At least have your publicist try," I say, the pup reminding me of Cupcake.

Dylan took such sweet care of that dog. Just like he took care of me.

Feeding me, helping me with lab work, planning adventures, and comforting me on the toilet weren't part of our bargain. Those were things he chose to do, and why would he do those things unless he cared? At least a little?

Maybe Carrie and I went racing off into the forest after the wrong fox. We spent all of two seconds discussing option one, the possibility that Dylan has more-than-friends feelings, too. He could. It's not beyond the realm of possibility. And don't I owe it to both of us to find out?

I mean, hell, we all have issues.

That doesn't mean we're lost causes or incapable of love.

I don't want to give up on Dylan so easily, not even if it means ruining any chance of returning to our friends-with-baby-making-benefits arrangement.

I stay up late Sunday night, tucked into Carrie's guest room, writing draft after draft of one of the scariest things I've ever put on paper. Early Monday morning on my way back into Mercyville, I slip the letter into the Hunter family mailbox, cross my fingers, and hope I haven't thrown the baby away with the bathwater.

CHAPTER 19

DYLAN

*I*t's been four days since we spoke. Four days since I've touched her, smelled her, tasted her. Four days of torture, spent watching her working in her garden and walking her property with her vineyard manager and riding her bike to town looking cute as fuck in a fuzzy orange hat and a matching scarf that trails behind her in the breeze as she rides.

Four days of radio silence during which my phone has not received a single call or text. And yeah, I haven't reached out, either, but *I'm* the one who apologized and begged her to stay at the harvest parade. I'm the one who rolled over and showed his underbelly and was told "see you around, I need space and time."

The ball is in her court. If she decides she's done playing, then that's it.

It's over. Done. Finished.

I let out a string of obscenities, barely resisting the urge to hurl the hoe I'm trying to reattach to its handle out the barn window and then kick the fuck out of the broken lawn mower for good measure.

"Easy there, son." My dad's voice comes from the hayloft, making me flinch.

"Shit, you scared me." I turn, glancing up toward the roof of the barn, where my old man is sitting in a makeshift throne of hay bales, whittling. "How long have you been lurking up there?"

"I'm not lurking. I'm enjoying some peace and quiet." Dad casts a glance down his nose. "Or I was until you had your temper tantrum."

"I'm not having a temper tantrum. I'm just fucking sick of broken things." I toss the hoe onto the dirt floor by the shovel the boys ran over with my truck on their way to school because they refuse to put things back where they found them.

"Aren't we all? But broken things are a part of life, and bitching doesn't help them get fixed any faster."

"Someone's philosophical all of a sudden," I mutter, digging through a box of old engine parts, looking for something I can use to patch up the lawnmower for a few more runs. It's almost time for the grass to go dormant. If it can limp along another few weeks, I'll have three months without pasture mowing to save for a replacement.

"Yeah, well, I've been doing some thinking lately." The sound of Dad's knife softly *snicking* at the wood fills the silence as he pauses for a long moment. Long enough that I've almost forgotten what we were talking about when he adds, "And I've been seeing that lady my doctor said I should talk to. The one with the office in Sebastopol."

My hand goes still and the record of grievances playing in my head screeches to a stop. I stand, propping my hands on my hips as I give my old my man my full attention. "Seriously? The therapist? You went?"

He nods, his gaze still fixed on his work. "I did. Twice. And going back again next Wednesday."

I blink. "Wow. Well, good… I'm glad, Dad. I know you're tough as nails, but coming back from cancer is hard. I'm glad you've found something that's helping."

"It's not just the cancer," he says mildly. "It's other stuff, too, things I've been going about the wrong way, maybe. Certainly not the best way." He pauses again, letting his work drop to his lap as he meets my gaze. "I'd like to apologize for being so hard on you, Dylan. You did the best you could, and you provided for the family when I couldn't. I've been looking for someone to blame so I can stay angry instead of admitting that life as I knew it is over and moving on. I'm sorry."

I'm pretty sure my eyes are bulging out of my head at this point, and I certainly have no idea what to say to this man who is speaking at a reasonable volume and talking sense.

So I just nod and mumble, "S'okay, Dad. We're good."

"I hope we are," he says. "Because I love you, and I'm proud of you."

I take a deep breath and hold it, shocked by the wave of emotion rushing through me. I want to say thank you, but I'm afraid if I talk I'll do something embarrassing like get all fucking teary about my old man telling me he loves me. I know that he loves me, I've always known it, but after all the shit he's been shoveling my way the past few months, it sure is nice to hear.

"And I want you to forget about the pumpkin patch," he continues. "I'm too old to be planting new vines, anyway. No need to put the family deeper in debt to get more land, when what we've got is working out just fine."

My breath rushes out with a sigh. It's feels like someone kicked the chopping block out from under my head and reached a hand down to help me up. "Thanks, Dad. Seriously. That's...a load off."

"But that doesn't mean you should stop seeing that girl," he adds. "In fact, I think you should drop what you're doing and go pay her a visit right now. You were a lot more pleasant to be around when you were sleeping over at her place."

"Maybe I'll go see your therapist instead," I deflect, not wanting to talk about Emma with Dad, not when I'm feeling all warm and fuzzy and in the mood to forget how Pop's lax attitude about getting women pregnant negatively impacted my life.

"I can fix the lawnmower," he says, ignoring my jab, "and grab a hoe when I'm at the hardware store later. Go see your lady. You'll both feel better after, I'm sure."

"She's not my lady." I cross my arms over my chest as I rock back onto the heels of my work boots. "And I can't go see her. She wants to take a break."

Pop frowns hard. "Why on earth would she want to do that? You weren't being selfish in the bedroom, were you? I thought I raised you boys better than that. She comes first. Always."

"I'm not going to talk about that with you," I say with a hard eye roll. "But no, I wasn't being selfish. That was...all good. She just changed her mind about having a child who will never know his or her extended family, I guess." I shrug, pretending getting cut off from Emma doesn't feel like banishment to the shittiest level of hell. "Which is probably good. It was a weird arrangement, anyway."

"What was weird about it?" Pop huffs. "You were falling in love while trying to make a baby. Sounds like the most natural thing in the world to me."

I shake my head. "It wasn't like that. We're just friends. That's what she wanted, so...that's what we are. Or were."

He grunts, lips turning down. "Well, then. Guess I misunderstood things."

That makes two of us. I suspected Emma and I weren't on the same page emotionally, but I never imagined she would be able to walk away from me, just like that, no looking back. It makes me doubt my own sanity. Did I imagine all the fun we had? The way we laughed and talked and made love until I felt so close to her I believed I could tell her anything? Confess all my secret hopes and dreams—with the exception of one, of course.

And thank God I held that one back, or I'd be even more ashamed of myself than I am already.

"But I will tell you this..." Dad adds as he holds his piece of wood up to the light, studying his work. "Both of the women I married were friends first. There's no better recipe for love that lasts than friendship mixed with a healthy dose of chemistry. If Nancy and I had been as good at fidelity as we were at fornicating and being friends, you, Rafe, and Tristan would never have been born."

I shove my hands into my back pockets. "I didn't know Nancy cheated, too." Dad doesn't talk much about his first wife, Deacon's mom.

"She did," Dad says mildly, clearly no longer upset about it. "She cheated first, then I had my revenge plus a couple of free passes I thought I deserved, and the trust spiraled down the drain from there." He nods my way before resuming dragging his blade across the wood. "But you're not me. And Emma isn't anyone but herself. And it sounds to me like the two of you have something worth hanging onto."

"This was your plan all along, wasn't it?" I ask, suspicion blooming in my brain. "You were never on board with the 'knock her up and send her on her way' plan. You wanted me to get hooked on this woman."

Dad's squints down at the wood in his hands. "Oh, I don't know about hooked. When Stroker and I met her that first weekend, right after she moved in, we might have noticed that she was cute as a button, as sweet as all get out, and seemed almost as lonely as you've been the past few years. But we had no way of knowing you two would hit it off this well…"

"So, Mr. Stroker's in on this, too?" I pace across the dirt floor and back again. "He was never considering selling to Emma, was he? He was just dragging it out to throw the two of us together."

"Well, guess you're as smart as all your teachers said you were, aren't you?" Dad makes a half-hearted attempt to hide his smile, but he's too damned proud of himself to do a decent job. "Sorry again about giving you a hard time about the pumpkin patch. I wanted to make sure you stayed invested, but I didn't mean to be a thorn in your side."

I huff and pace faster, not knowing whether to be pissed that I was so easily played or...grateful.

Grateful that someone stepped in and saved me from my bad habit of pushing people away before they can complicate my already complicated life. If Pop or anyone else had tried to set me up with Emma, I would have had my walls up so fast there would have been no way in hell even someone as amazing as she is could have tempted me to drop a drawbridge.

But throwing us together in competition over a piece of land, making me notice her as a rival first...

Well, I guess it says something about me that I'm more open to intimacy with someone who's messing with my well-laid plans than a woman I think I could fall for. Something not great.

But now the woman I couldn't stand has become someone I can't stand to lose. The thought of never fucking her again is torturous, yes. But the thought of never having an adventure day with her, or sharing a meal with her, or hearing her laugh that wild giggle I've only heard when she's with me—all of those things hurt just as much. More.

In just three weeks, she's gotten under my skin, in my head, and oh-so-close to my heart. And the world hasn't come to an end. I'm not any more or less trapped in this life I'm ready to change than I was before.

Suddenly my refusal to consider a serious relationship—or even date the same woman for more than a month or two at a time—seems ridiculous. Falling for Emma isn't going to put a wrench in my plans, not as long as I can convince her that I'm worth putting some of her other plans on hold.

I stop dead in the middle of the barn, squinting at the "I like big cows and I cannot lie; you udder brothers can't deny" poster the twins hung on the wall above Moo-donna's stall, as if the answer to the burning question setting fire to my thoughts will be found in the calm brown gaze of the steer staring into the camera.

"If you're wondering how to apologize to a woman," Dad pipes up, still scratching away, "then I'm your man. My marriages both lasted years longer than they should have, and I credit that to my skill with an apologetic turn of phrase."

I shake my head. "Thanks, but no thanks, Dad. I'm good with apologies. I need something more than that. I need—"

"You need to sweep the lady off her feet," Rafe says from the entrance to the barn, grinning as he nods back toward the house. "Come with me, grasshopper. Allow me to instruct you in the fine art of romancing the fuck out of the fairer sex. I've got some other stuff I wanted to discuss with you, anyway."

"But keep it genuine, Rafe," Dad calls after us. "This

is the real deal. Dylan doesn't want to let this girl get away."

I smile, knowing better than to deny it. Not to Pop, not to Rafe, and not to myself. No more keeping quiet or letting Emma walk away without a fight. Time to be that knight on a white horse she was tired of waiting for.

Because I'm tired of waiting, too.

CHAPTER 20

EMMA

ednesday dawns grey and cold, with rain drooling from the sky in a steady stream that does not bode well for my first wine road event.

By the time I've finished my first cup of coffee, the driveway has gone from soggy to imitating a small mountain stream, and I curse myself for putting off the gravel delivery until later in the month. The chance an oversize tour bus toting drunk San Franciscans will get stuck in the mud outside my tasting room is increasing with every passing second, and the sober expression on Bart's usually sunny face as he lays out sandbags in an attempt to divert the worst of the runoff isn't encouraging.

But the show must go on.

The Wine and Wonder event is the biggest of the season and a chance to put Haverford Estates on the map. Everything has to be perfect, or as perfect as I can make it, considering the miserable weather and the fact that I've been down in the dumps since Monday night.

He hasn't texted.

He hasn't called.

He hasn't so much as paused to glance my way while out and about on his property.

And I've been watching. Boy, have I been watching. I've been following Dylan's movements like a chocoholic tracking the last dark chocolate truffle at the party, making sure I'm in my garden when he's doing chores, peering at him from under my straw hat, waiting for a sign that he's considering all the things I said in my letter. But with every passing day, becoming more than friends, or even picking up where we left off, is looking more and more unlikely.

And that hurts. Concrete block dropped on my heart level of hurt.

I've always enjoyed alone time, but it's torturous to me now. Eating alone, reading after dinner alone, going to bed alone, wishing I hadn't washed my sheets so that they would still smell like Dylan....

Long story short—I miss him. So much.

My house is haunted with memories of our time together. Hell, the entire town is haunted. I can't even enjoy a coffee at Barn Roasters without keeping one eye trained on the door, waiting for Dylan to walk in.

But he hasn't been in for coffee since our argument Saturday night, a major shift in behavior that proves how determined he is to avoid me. He's willing to give up one of his favorite simple pleasures just so he won't have to look at my stupid face.

"Your face is not stupid," I mutter as I brush on eye shadow, hoping the glittery silver color will lift my spirits. "Your heart is stupid for getting so attached to him, and your brain is stupid for coming up with this plan in the first place."

But at least you make good wine, I tell myself, determined to get my head in the right place for the long weekend ahead. The Wine and Wonder event runs through Sunday, and we're expecting between three and five hundred visitors, which means I'm on deck to work the tasting room with Denver and Neil to help manage the increased traffic.

And to smooth feathers in case we're forced to deny someone a tasting.

The more experienced winery owners warned me at the planning meeting that event days can get ugly by two or three o'clock, when people have been tasting since ten in the morning and many haven't stopped to eat a proper lunch. If someone is visibly inebriated or belligerent, it's my job to make sure they aren't served.

Needless to say, I'm not looking forward to playing bad cop. Conflict isn't my strong suit on a good day, when the person I'm disagreeing with is sober.

Which reminds me...

I shoot off a quick text to Carrie, even though I know she's on a plane to a writer's conference and won't be able to answer—

· · ·

EMMA: Just discovered another layer to my shit sandwich—dealing with drunk people at public events. Wish me luck.

—AND HEAD OUT THE DOOR, holding my raincoat over my head as I dash the twenty feet from the house to the entrance to the tasting room.

Inside, blond and ridiculously gorgeous Neil is looking stressed. His usually perfectly-feathered hair sticks up in frizzed waves on one side as he unloads bottles of Pinot Noir behind the wooden bar spanning the length of the stable house turned tasting room.

"Oh thank God." His shoulders sag in relief as I step inside, hanging my coat on one of the antique hooks on the wall. "You're here. You'll fix it."

"Fix what?" I ask, crossing to the bar.

"The labels on the new cases are wrong." He plunks a bottle of Pinot on the reclaimed wood between us and jabs a finger at the golden script on the label. "They all say Chardonnay."

"Oh my God." I shake my head as I lean in for a closer look. "How did that happen?"

"Mix up at the bottling facility, I'm betting." Denver cruises in from the stock room with another case of wine in his arms, his dark hair pulled back into a braid instead of his usual smooth ponytail. "The Chardonnay is all labeled Pinot, too. I just checked. They must have popped the wrong stack of labels into the machine."

I curse softly and chew the edge of my thumb,

thinking fast. "And we don't have any properly labeled bottles?"

"Not here," Denver says, setting the second mismatched case by my feet. "We might have some in the warehouse, assuming the bottlers didn't fuck them all up."

"Surely they didn't." I rake a hand through my hair and fist it, knowing I have to make a call and make it quick. We only have an hour before go time.

"Okay," I say, breath rushing out. "Here's what we'll do—Neil, go ahead and get two tasting stations set up with the mismatched bottles, and add in the Sauvignon Blanc so we'll have at least one offering that is what it says it is. Denver, get the truck keys from Bart and head to the warehouse. They open at ten. I'll call Misty and tell her to be expecting you. Hopefully she can get you what you need ASAP, then you can load up fast and be back here before noon."

"And if the bottles at the warehouse are all mixed up, too?" he asks, backing toward the door.

"Don't put that out into the universe, Denver. They're going to be fine." I point a stern finger his way, only for my elbow to sag with doubt as he arches a skeptical brow. "But if they're wrong, too, stop by the craft store and get some silver permanent markers to write on the bottles, and we'll improvise."

Denver claps his hands together. "Got it, boss."

"And what about the cheese puff pastries?" Neil asks.

"What about them?" I glance down at my watch. "They were supposed to go into the oven at nine. Tell me you put them in, Neil."

"I did put them in, but they're not going to cook as long as the power's out in the stock room and kitchen."

"What?" I screech, my pitch high enough to make poor Neil wince. "When did this happen?"

"About thirty minutes ago," he says. "I'm sorry. I thought Bart told you."

I sigh. "He's been trying to keep the driveway from washing away. I'm sure he just forgot. Let me run the pastries into the house and put them on in there. Then we can load them into the cupcake carrier and ferry them back and forth to keep them dry."

It's a solid plan, but some days it doesn't matter if you have a solid plan. The powers that be are out to get you, and all your puny human efforts to thwart fate simply make them laugh.

Laugh and then laugh some more when you hurry off the porch with the last load of pastries and slip in a patch of mud, going down hard, smearing the back of your gray linen pants with clay caked an inch deep.

I groan, cringing as I stand and my backside still feels like I'm sitting in an inch of freezing rainwater. But at least the cupcake carrier full of pastries landed right side up on the porch.

Thanking the universe for small miracles, and waddling to avoid disrupting the mud caked on the inside of my thighs, I make my way inside in time to see Neil turn bright red and press a fist to his mouth.

"What's wrong?" I ask, eyes wide.

"Mushrooms," he wheezes, hand coming to clutch his throat. "You said they were cheese pastries. You didn't say anything about mushrooms. I'm allergic to mushrooms."

"Shit, what do I do? Call 911?" Launching into motion, I hurry around the bar toward the phone, but Neil is already circling around the other way.

"No, I just need Benadryl. I usually have some with me, but I forgot my man purse at Steve's last night after I left early because we were fighting about dumb shit." He coughs, then violently clears his throat. "If I die, I'm going to come back and haunt his ass for killing me by insisting we can't go to the same ski lodge two years in a row. Do you think Bart can drive me to the pharmacy?"

"Just head into my master bath," I say, pointing urgently toward the house. "I have Benadryl in the medicine cabinet. Pills and liquid for when I need the allergy pain to stop faster."

"Bless you," Neil croaks, clearly relieved. "I'll be back as soon as I don't feel like I'm going to pass out or swell up. You've got this, boss. Don't worry. Just take your time and move methodically down the line. They shouldn't be rabid for a pour this early in the day."

Before I can ask him what he's talking about, he hurries outside, the door swinging wide behind him to reveal a giant bus parking in my one and only bus parking spot and shutting off its engine.

"Shit," I curse, pulse hammering with anxiety as I grab a roll of paper towels from near the washing machine and swipe at the mess on my backside.

I have just enough time to realize that my swiping is making things worse—and causing a very poo-esque earthworm smell to rise from my damp slacks—when the first tasters push through the door. Plastering what I'm sure is a hysterical grin on my face, I shove the dirty towels in the trash, wash my hands as fast as humanly possible, say a prayer that no one will notice my messy bottom or unpleasant odor, and start lining up glasses and handing out tasting menus.

I've got the first fifteen or sixteen folks set up, and have managed to flip on my favorite tasting playlist—good music trumps bad smells, right?—and am feeling like I might squeak through this without crashing and burning when a familiar laugh sounds from near the door.

It's still *so* familiar, even though I didn't hear much of it in our final months together, when my fiancé was so busy sneaking around and sticking his penis into other people that the stress of juggling his romantic entanglements affected his sense of humor.

But you don't forget a booming, Santa-Claus belly laugh like Jeremy's.

It's him, no doubt in my mind. I know it instantly, even before I turn, time slowing to a horror-movie crawl as I pull six-foot-two Jeremy and his much shorter friend into focus.

Veronica is here, too, even though she's so pregnant her swollen belly strains the front of her dress, jutting out into the crowd like the bow of a ship cutting smoothly through the water, clearing a path to the bar. She's wearing ruby-red jeweled barrettes that match the flowers on her dress in her dark brown hair, and her olive skin is glowing like she's been lit up from the inside.

She was always beautiful, but now she is stunning, vibrant, the creating and incubating of life clearly agreeing with her in every way.

It's enough to make me want to throw a wine bottle through the window to my right, launch myself through it, and run away through the rain sobbing hysterically.

But I can't. Denver is off property, Neil is guzzling Benadryl in my bathroom, and Bart is too busy with sandbags to take over for me, even if he weren't vehemently opposed to talking to strangers.

Nope. There's no way out of this.

It's just me, and my soggy mud butt, alone.

And I will have to face this, face *him*, look up into the brown eyes of the man who betrayed me so completely it took months to stitch together the tattered scraps of my self worth, pour him wine, and pretend everything is fine, even if it kills me.

Now. I have to do it now. There's not another second to waste if I want to have these people out before the next batch of tasting enthusiasts arrive.

I turn toward the other side of the bar, chilled bottle of Sauvignon Blanc clutched in hand, feeling like a monster claw is clutching at my throat at the same time.

Not just clutching but squeezing, making my pulse race and my stomach threaten to bring up the biscuit I had for breakfast. I'm still several feet from my destination when black prickles begin to dance at the edge of my vision and my head informs me that it will be floating off my body and will return later, when all of these horrible people are gone.

I realize I'm about to faint, and throw out a hand,

leaning against the heavily stocked shelves behind the bar. I close my eyes and pull in a deep breath, willing myself to stay upright.

I can't faint. I refuse to let Jeremy see me go down, to give him any reason to think I'm still the broken person who sobbed on our couch for hours after learning my fiancé had knocked up another woman. I have to keep going, stay strong, because there is no one here to help and no one to catch me if I fall.

"Hey, what's going on? Why are you in here all alone on an event day?" another familiar voice asks from so close I can smell his heavenly scent drifting to my nose on the damp breeze blowing through the window.

My eyes fly open to see Dylan ducking under the closed flap at the center of the bar, holding the most beautiful arrangement of flowers I've ever seen, and my heart explodes with relief. It doesn't matter that we fought, or haven't spoken in days, one look in his eyes and I know that he's here for me, the way he has been since that night in the woods, proving there are still heroes left in the world.

"Everything has gone to shit," I whisper softly. "The labels are mixed up, Denver had to run to town, Neil is sick, the power is out in the tasting room kitchen, and I fell on my butt running cheese pastries over from the house."

Concern flashes across his face. "You okay?"

"Physically, yes. Mentally, been better, and emotionally in the crapper." I force a smile as I motion over his shoulder with the top of the bottle in my hand. "The tall guy at the end of the bar is my ex. The pregnant woman next to him is the woman he left me for. This will be the first time I've spoken to him since the day he called off our engagement, and my head is trying to float off my body to avoid it."

"Like hell you're talking to him." Dylan's scowl is stormier than the weather outside. He lays the flowers on the bar and pushes up the sleeves of his dark green sweater. "I'll pour for that side of the bar. You stay on that side and don't so much as look over your shoulder. That lying, cheating, sack of human garbage doesn't deserve to see you upset."

Gratitude swelling inside me like a puff pastry rising in a toasty oven, I press the bottle of white into Dylan's hand. "Bless you. Thank you. So much."

"My pleasure, Blondie. But before we pour, I need one thing."

Before I can promise to give him whatever he wants —no favor is too great in exchange for his life-saving heroism in the face of my evil ex—he wraps his free hand around my waist and pulls me close, fusing his lips to mine.

And then he kisses me in a way I've never been kissed before. Not even by him, the best kisser to ever press his mouth to mine.

He kisses me like he's been lost, and only now that he's back in my arms is he found. He kisses me like I'm the answer and the question and every magical step of the journey in between. His kiss is a promise, an invitation, a challenge I never expected from him, this man who seems so determined not to make his life any more complicated than it has to be.

And love is complicated. At least, that's what Jeremy and the other losers I've hooked up with through the years taught me to believe.

But maybe it doesn't have to be.

Maybe, when it's right, it's easy, like tasting cheese and eating ice cream and soaking in a perfect sunset.

By the time he pulls away, I don't feel like I'm going to faint. I don't feel scared or trapped or exposed. I feel safe, shot through with sparkles, and not at all alone.

"Talk later?" He cups my face in his hand, brushing his thumb gently across my bottom lip. "Once we get these losers out of here?"

"Yes," I say. "But don't call them losers. I would like to sell some wine today."

"Don't worry, baby. I'm going to sell the shit out your fine-ass wine. I'm a killer salesman when I believe in the product." He winks before nodding toward the shelves. "And those flowers are for you. I've got some really bad poetry I wrote to recite for you, too, but that will have to wait until we're alone."

I grin. "Sounds good."

It sounds better than good, it sounds like a big dream coming true.

With a final squeeze of my hand, Dylan heads toward the opposite side of the room, and I return to my post, pouring Chardonnay for the people who are ready to move on to the next wine. In between pouring and answering questions, I slice the cheese puffs into thirds, arrange them on tasting plates and pass them out to the people on my side of the bar in advance of the

Pinot, which pairs beautifully with the rich cheese and earthy mushrooms in the pastry.

Amazingly, I don't spare Jeremy and Veronica a second thought until it's time to deliver pastry samples to where Dylan is working the bar like a champ, making small talk about the area and the history of Green Valley wine as he pours.

I clench my jaw, preparing to act surprised, but not displeased, to see them, but when I reach Dylan's side, the spot where Jeremy and Veronica were standing is empty.

"Cheese puffs to go with the Pinot." I set the tray on the shelf behind him before adding in a softer voice, "What happened to you know who?"

Dylan shrugs, focus trained on the Pinot he's uncorking. "I don't know. The guy glared at me like I kicked his cat and stole his Bible and stomped out. Guess he didn't care for what we were pouring."

I grip his arm, fingers digging into his bicep as I whisper, "Thank you. I'm so happy I could just bite you. All over."

He shoots a heated glance my way. "I've noticed that about you. That you like to bite things when you're happy. Especially when you're *really* happy."

His tone leaves no doubt what he's talking about, making my cheeks flush.

"But that's one of the things I love about you," he adds, the look in his eyes assuring me that, this time, the words aren't a slip of the tongue.

The warm flush spreads to encompass my entire being. I want to tell him that I feel the same way, that

I'm crazy about him and so grateful that he showed up in my tasting room and in my bed and in my life, and that I don't ever want to fight again.

But before I can say a word, he leans in, kissing my forehead. "Now get out of here and let me pour the Pinot, before I drag you into the stock room, rip off your clothes, and have my way with you. Four days without you did a number on my impulse control."

"Yes, sir." Grinning, I give a little salute and hurry back to pour second tastings, fill orders, bag up wine, and run credit cards.

By the time the bus pulls away, we've sold twenty-five bottles.

"Amazing start!" Neil breezes back into the tasting room just as two limos are pulling up outside. "Seriously great. Especially for a winery that's hard to get to on a rainy day. I feel good things in our future today." He pauses to cast some serious side-eye at the puff pastries. "Assuming you keep those far away from me."

"Will do," I say, edging toward the door. "Dylan do you mind sticking around for a few more minutes while I run and change?"

"I'm here for as long as you need me, baby," he says, making my heart flip-flop all over again.

"Aw, you two," Neil says, clasping his hands together beneath his chin. "I'm so glad you're going public! It was such a drag pretending not to know you were coupling up behind the scenes." He sighs, then claps swiftly before jabbing a finger at Dylan. "Now get those glasses in the dishwasher, friend. We've got less than a minute to set up for the next group."

The people keep coming, wave after wave, until we run out of puff pastries and sell our last case of Sauvignon Blanc. Denver returns at noon with properly labeled bottles—thank God—just as the sky clears and the crowds begin to grow even thicker. Denver, Neil, Dylan, and I are all running at maximum capacity, pouring, cleaning, resetting, selling, and repeating, proving I vastly underestimated my staffing needs. I place a call to a winemaker friend during my late lunch break, securing two of her part-time tasting room employees for the rest of the event weekend, and have just enough time to heave a sigh of relief before I head back into the fray.

By five o'clock, we're all worn out, but there's no doubt that, despite the rocky start, our first day was a rousing success.

"You were a life saver." Denver claps Dylan on the back as we get the last stragglers out the door minutes before five. "Seriously, man. Appreciate the help."

"My pleasure," Dylan says, capturing my hand as he backs toward the house. "See you all around."

Before Neil or Denver can respond, Dylan has turned and practically dragged me onto the porch. I pick up my pace to catch up and he breaks into a jog. By the time we reach the door, we're both running. We tumble through, laughing as he slams it behind us, and then we come together with twin moans of relief that prove how glad we both are that our suffering is over.

We're together again. Truly together this time. And just like Neil, I feel good things in the future.

All good things.

CHAPTER 21

DYLAN

I don't want to talk; I want to kiss her. Everywhere. From her sweet lips to the curve of her hip to her tiny feet with the crooked big toes that are the cutest things I've ever seen. Every part of her is perfect, beautiful, unique, and precious, and all I want to do is show her how much I treasure every inch of her.

But before we get any more naked, I need her to understand how things have changed for me.

"Wait, baby," I say, the words ending in a groan as she shoves my boxers down my thighs, freeing my aching cock as we tumble onto the bed.

"No waiting," she says, kissing me hard. "I need you. I've missed you so much."

She's already naked, and it would be so easy to spread her thighs and sink inside her, take her bare, fuck her until we both come so hard we see stars, and put off worrying about the consequences. But she deserves better than that, and I can't roll those dice, not when keeping Emma here with me is starting to feel vital to my very survival.

My breath rushes out against her lips. "Me, too, but we have to talk first."

"About what?" Her nails skim down my back in a way that makes my balls throb.

"I need to use a condom," I say. "Tonight, and every night for the near future."

Her brow furrows and hurt flashes in her eyes.

I hurry to clarify, since hurting her is the last thing I want to do. "Things have changed since we started this. I know you feel it, too. This isn't a bargain between two friends anymore. This is me, wanting you to be mine. Hoping you want me to be yours. Because I—" I take a breath, man the fuck up, and speak the truth. "Because I'm falling in love with you, and I don't want to stop."

"I don't want you to stop," she whispers, eyes shining as she brushes my hair from my forehead. "I'm falling in love with you, too. Nothing felt right when you were gone. I was going crazy. All I wanted to do was hear your voice, but you never called."

I shake my head. "I thought you didn't want me to call. On Saturday, you said you needed space."

"But then I decided space was stupid and I needed you in my life and we should talk. Didn't you get my letter?" she asks, brow furrowing. "I put it in your mailbox Monday morning, on my way to get coffee."

I exhale, relief spreading through me. "No, we never check the mailbox. I had so much trouble getting Dad to remember to hand over the bills that we got separate post office boxes in town. Even the twins have one so they can get mail from Deacon."

"Oh thank God." She hugs me tight, pressing her breasts to my chest, making my heart beat faster. "I thought you were deliberately blowing me off. I thought I'd imagined that we were at least becoming good friends, and it was driving me crazy."

"Me, too," I say, throat going tight as she wraps her legs around my waist and my suffering length brushes against where she's hot and ready for me. I swallow hard, fighting for control. "Condom, Emma. I need to get one. I don't want to knock you up until we're both ready to be parents. Together. But I'm not sure how much longer I can resist, baby." I groan as she rocks against me, hips lifting to meet my throbbing cock. "I'm dying to be inside you, to make you come for me."

"Yes." Feathering kisses across my face, she flails an arm toward the bedside table. "Top drawer. In the back. I have some in there."

In seconds, I've got the package open, then a condom on, and then I'm pushing inside where I've been dying to be, coming home as I glide deep into my girl. And the physical sensation isn't the same with the condom, that's a damned fact, but the connection I feel as I catch and hold Emma's gaze while I move inside her is more intense than ever before.

There's no more hiding, no more worry. I'm free to make love to her, to worship shamelessly at the altar of her body *and* her heart, and by the time we lose control together, coming within seconds of each other as her legs lock tight around me, I'm even more crazy about her than I was before.

"I'm falling in love with you, princess," I confess as we lie fused together, catching our breath.

"Me, too. With you," she says, communicating love with every brush of her hand up and down my back.

I swear I can feel it in a way I thought was fairy tale crazy before her.

Pressing a grateful kiss onto her forehead, I pull away, make quick work of the condom, and return to bed, crawling under the covers and pulling Emma close.

She comes eagerly, arm wrapping around my ribs as her cheek rests on my chest. "This is so much nicer," she says with a sigh. "I was getting so tired of pretending I didn't love snuggling you as much as the other stuff."

I run a hand over her soft curls. "Me, too. And I know you're ready to have a baby, but I confess I'm glad Operation Sperm Donor didn't work out. In theory, I thought I could handle it… But it would have haunted me, knowing you were out there somewhere with our baby and I wasn't a part of your lives. I'm just not ready."

"I understand." She lifts her head, meeting my gaze in the fading light. "I truly do. And I know it's early days for us as more than friends, but I… Well…"

"Spit it out, Blondie," I urge. "You can tell me anything. I want you to be honest with me. For us to be honest with each other from here on out."

She nods, gaze falling to the rumpled covers. "I'd just like to know if you think children will ever be on the horizon for you. If they are, I can wait, see if this works out between us. I have some wiggle room biological-clock wise." She pulls in a breath, fingertips brushing back and forth across my chest. "But I don't know if I can give up the dream of babies forever, even for something as good as this."

"I understand. And yeah, I think I want kids. Someday. It's just a lot to wrap my head about right now with everything else that's going on. You and me becoming you and me, and Rafe and I moving out of the farmhouse."

Emma looks up, eyes wide. "You're moving? Where?"

"Not far. Just to Santa Rosa. Rafe found a space downtown that's perfect for what we both need," I say, unable to keep the excitement from my voice. But then, Emma doesn't care about playing it cool. "There's enough room in the retail area for motorcycle sales and beer tasting, with plenty of space in the back for Rafe's repair work and my brewery equipment. And there's a two-bedroom apartment upstairs, so zero commute."

"That's amazing," Emma says with a big smile. "So you're going for it. Making the brewery dream come true."

I laugh softly. "Yeah, I hope so. We'll see if I'm any good at making beer on that scale. I've been making home brew for years, but nothing this big."

"You'll make amazing beer. No doubt in my mind. And I love the idea of combining motorcycle sales and a brewery. They fit together perfectly, right?"

"That's what Rafe and I are thinking." I run some of our early marketing ideas past Emma as my hand drifts down to her ass, cupping the firm mound I've missed so much the past few days.

"Sounds solid." She tips her head to one side as she bemusedly studies my face. "Patting my ass really does help you think, doesn't it?"

I grin and give her cheek a squeeze. "I told you, butt-fondling gives me great ideas. Like taking you on a tour of my new place after you're done in the tasting room tomorrow." I brush a lock of hair from her face. "And then we can stop by the hardware store and get a key made for you. I want you to come over and let yourself in any time."

"Sounds perfect." She leans in, kissing me soft and sweet. "I'll get a key made for you, too."

Exchanging keys.

It's not making a baby, but it's a big step, one that feels so right I'm hard again in seconds.

Soon Emma's breasts are in my hands and her breath is coming faster as our kisses grow deep, desperate. We break apart long enough for Emma to grab a condom and roll it on my length, and then my hands are around her waist, guiding her down onto me, rocking into her as she rides me with languid strokes of her hips that drive me wild.

This woman makes me so hot for her, but it's the look in her eyes that breaks my heart wide open. She's all in, hiding nothing, giving me every piece of her, trusting that I'll handle her with care.

And I will, I swear it to myself and to her, my voice rough with the effort it's taking not to come too fast. "I love you, baby. So much. I promise you won't regret this."

"Never," she says, breasts rising and falling faster as she nears the edge. "Never. Oh God, Dylan. I'm so close…"

I groan as she rocks faster, making my balls tighten as I reach the edge of my own release. And then her spine arches and her head falls back as she comes so hard I can feel every pulse of her body, even through the latex between us.

A beat later, I'm gone.

"Yes, Emma. God…" I grip her hips tight, pinning her to me as I come, pulsing deep inside her. "You're so beautiful when you come for me. So perfect."

And she is.

This is.

I've never been with someone who made falling in love feel so effortless.

We spend the rest of the night eating sandwiches in her kitchen, taking a glass of wine into bed, and talking until it's pitch black outside and the night sky is full of stars. We make love again, slow and close, with her spooned against me as I glide in and out of her from behind, and though I miss taking her bare, I know this is for the best.

We're on the right track now. I feel it in my bones, in my gut, in my heart that is oh-so-quickly becoming hers to do with as she pleases.

The thought would have scared me once, but not now. I trust Emma and she trusts me, and it's going to be nothing but smooth sailing from here on out.

I truly believe that, right up until the moment I arrive at Emma's house on Thursday evening, ready to take her on a tour of my new digs, only to find her gone, her drawers empty, and a note with my name on it lying on the bed.

CHAPTER 22

EMMA

*T*urn *around! Go home! Stop the insanity before it's too late!*

But it's already too late.

It was too late last night, but of course I didn't know that when I was making Dylan promises I won't be able to keep.

I didn't know the truth until nine thirty this morning when, instead of dashing out the door to the tasting room, I was dashing into the bathroom to throw up everything I'd eaten for breakfast...

I CURSE SOFTLY as I sit back against the shower door and pull my phone from my jeans pocket. When Carrie answers, I don't bother with formalities, "Don't come up today. Stay home. I'm sick and I don't want to infect you if I'm contagious."

"Oh no," Carrie says. "Bummer. I was looking forward to

seeing you and watching the magic happen in the tasting room."

"Me, too." I sigh. "But I just finished being sick, and I know how much you hate vomit. I feel better now, so it might just be a touch of food poisoning, but—"

"Or a touch of knocked up," she cuts in, making me blink in surprise. "You've heard of morning sickness, right?"

"Of course," I say with a shaky laugh. "But I just had my period. There's no way I'm pregnant."

"But you said it was super light, right? I remember you did, because it made me think I should keep an eye on you, just in case. My friend Casey from college spotted all through her pregnancy. She didn't even realize she was knocked up until she was almost five months along. After she'd broken up with Gareth and had been drinking like a fish for weeks to drown the heartache. But the baby was fine. So don't worry if you've had a glass or two. I'm sure you'll both be fine."

I huff, shaking my head. "Good to know, but I'm not pregnant. I can't be." But even as I deny the possibility, my heart beats faster, and a wonderful, dreadful feeling rises inside of me.

If I'm pregnant, it will be a miracle, the answer to a prayer.

But if I'm pregnant it will also mean that Dylan won't have dodged that bullet after all. The one he made it clear he was so grateful to have avoided. He's not ready to become a father. He doesn't want this baby. And maybe he won't want me, either, once he realizes what's happened.

"Just take a test," Carrie says, her voice penetrating the panic and excitement coursing through me. "And then call me back. I want to be the first to know. And then we can talk about how you're going to break the news to Sexy Farmer."

"I'll take a test later today. I have to get to work right now," I lie, needing time to think before I commit to sharing this news—or lack of news; there's still an excellent chance I'm not pregnant—with anyone. Even my sister.

"Okay, but if I don't hear from you by tonight, I'm jumping in the car and coming up there to put a stick in your pee myself."

"Gross." My stomach snarls at the thought. But I don't feel sick. I just feel...empty, like I need a piece of bread or something to calm the stomach storm.

"This from the girl who showed me how to put in a tampon?" Carrie asks.

"That's different. That's big sister call of duty stuff." I come to my feet and head for the kitchen. "I'll call you later, okay? I promise."

As soon as I hang up with Carrie, I call Neil and tell him something's come up and I won't be able to make it to the tasting room until later. He assures me they'll be fine with the extra hands I called in, and the last obstacle to learning the truth ASAP is easily removed. I consider heading for the drugstore to grab an over the counter test, but in the end, I call Dr. Seal's office and make a ten-thirty appointment with the nurse practitioner, instead.

If I am pregnant, I need to know if the baby's okay—bleeding for several days doesn't seem like a good thing, even if it was a light flow—and they'll be able to do an ultrasound at the office.

I focus on making a logical decision and gathering data. I

do my best not to worry about Dylan or how a positive outcome might affect our future until I know for sure there's something to worry about.

I manage to stay relatively calm until approximately ten forty-eight a.m. when a transvaginal ultrasound reveals a tiny dot.

A tiny dot that is my baby.

My baby...

I'm pregnant...

I'm pregnant and the baby is just fine.

The nurse tells me that a little bleeding in the beginning is normal, but to come back in if I start bleeding again. She congratulates me, reminds me to keep taking my prenatal vitamins, gives me a list of foods I should avoid now that I'm pregnant, and sends me to the front desk to make my next appointment.

But I walk right past the front desk out to my car, where I sit in the parking lot for a solid half hour, devising a plan that I hope will make everything okay.

Or as okay as it can be considering I'm thrilled to the depths of my being at the news of this miracle baby, and the man I love doesn't want to be a father.

THREE HOURS LATER, I'm almost to Carrie's house, with enough clothes in my suitcase for several weeks, and half of my heart left behind me in Mercyville.

I have no idea if my plan is going to work, but I've done the best I can, and I can't bring myself to regret this life growing inside of me. I'm already in love with this tiny miracle human, willing to do whatever it takes to keep him or her healthy, happy, and safe.

Even if it means giving up the only man who ever made me feel loved for exactly who I am.

CHAPTER 23

*D*ear Dylan,

I'm so sorry. I hate to say one thing and then do another, but after thinking more about what we talked about last night, I realized I can't put off trying to become a mom for a year or more. Especially in light of the fact that you're not sure you want to have children someday. (Which I totally understand. I don't judge you at all for feeling the way you feel and wanting the things you want.)

But I'm older than you are, Cougar Bait, and I have fertility problems that may make it impossible for me to conceive if I wait. Believe me, if that weren't the case, I would absolutely wait, because you are worth waiting for. You are the kindest, sexiest, most thoughtful and fun man I know, and I'm honored that you want me to be your girl.

But a baby is one of my big dreams.

It's something I have to reach for with both hands. If I don't, regret will eat me up inside and make me unfit company for all the people I love. And I don't want that for them or for me.

Or for you.

I care so much about you, Dylan, and that's why I'm going to stay with my sister in Berkeley and work with a non-profit sperm bank near her house. I'm making the decision to try to become pregnant on my own so you won't feel pressured to make any commitments—or DNA contributions—you're not ready to make.

I'm trying to do what's best for both of us, but I understand if this changes your feelings about moving forward with a romantic relationship. Just know that I have treasured our time together so much.

You're so special to me and you always will be.

All my love,

Emma

I REREAD the note she left for the fifth time, but repetition doesn't make it any easier to take.

I pace the floor in front of the bed where we made love last night, feeling sick, frustrated, and so unexpectedly filled with rage I know I'm not going to be able to think this through rationally on my own. Not until the red haze has cleared, anyway.

But I don't have time to wait for the anger cloud to dissolve. With every passing minute, Emma is getting farther away from me, on her way to make a decision that feels more wrong with every repeat reading of her letter.

So I pull out my phone and call Tristan, hoping a calm head can help me sort out my next move.

He answers on the third ring, "Hey, Dylan. What's up?"

"A lot," I say, continuing to pace. "A hell of a lot, and I could use your advice."

I fill him in on the situation. By the time I reach the part about walking into Emma's place to find a note and no Emma, my pacing has expanded to the rest of the house. I prowl through cozy rooms that are empty and lifeless without Emma here to light them up, so worked up it feels like I'm about to come out of my skin.

"But this is a shitty decision," I continue. "What happens if the baby gets sick down the line? Or hurt in an accident? Or what if he or she needs blood or stem cells or God forbid, a kidney or something? That sperm donor is going to be exactly zero fucking help."

"True," Tristan says. "But I'm sure that's something Emma's considered. It sounds like she's trying to do the best she can considering the two of you are in such different places when it comes to having children."

"We're not in such different places," I snap back. "I just needed some time. Why couldn't she give me at least a few months?"

"Did you ask her for a few months?" Tristan asks, always ready to call me on my bullshit.

I sigh, bracing a hand on the back of the couch. "No. I didn't. I was vague as hell. But if I'd known she was going to do this…"

"If you had, you might have said something different, but would you have meant it?" Tristan prods. "There's no shame in not being ready, you know.

Having a child is the biggest commitment you can make. You're right to be taking it seriously."

"I know, but..." I shake my head, eyes closing. "But all I can think about... I keep seeing a little girl with blue eyes like Emma's lying in a hospital bed, and no matter how much we want to, there's nothing Emma or I can do to help her." I open my eyes, staring at the blood-red of the poppies stitched onto Emma's throw pillows. "Neither of us are a match for the kind of blood or whatever it is she needs, and we're just...fucking powerless. And I know that's worst-case scenario thinking and chances are nothing like will ever happen. But what if it does?"

Tristan is quiet for a long moment, but without him in the room, I have no idea if he's wearing his thinking face or has simply been rendered speechless by my crazy.

"You think I'm nuts, don't you?" I ask after several silent beats, pacing into Emma's office. "That I'm over-thinking the way I did when we were kids and I hid your dirt bike so you couldn't follow Rafe to the stunt track."

Tris laughs. "I forgot about that. God, I was so pissed at you when I found out."

"I was just trying to keep you safe," I say defensively.

"I know, and you were right. I would have busted my face. I could barely ride in a straight line at that point. But getting back to the matter at hand... I don't know if you're overthinking things, but the fact that in your imaginary scenario you and Emma are together at this little girl's bedside…" He pauses, giving his words time to hit.

And they do. Hard.

"The baby should be mine." The anger clouds evaporate as I achieve bright, crystal clear clarity. "I want to be the father of that child."

"Sure sounds like it," Tristan says. "But maybe you should take at least a day or two to think things over before you do anything rash."

I charge through the house, grabbing my jacket from the back of the couch on my way. "Like drive to Berkeley, find Emma's sister's place, and hold a boom box playing love songs up outside her window until she agrees that I'm the only one allowed to get her pregnant?"

"Yeah," Tristan says dryly. "Like that. You're already on your way out the door, aren't you?"

"Getting in the truck now," I say, slamming the door behind me.

He laughs. "Then good luck. It seems like Emma makes you happy. I hope you two can work everything out."

"Thanks, man. Talk to you later. I appreciate the advice." I end the call and roar up Emma's driveway, plotting the fastest route south.

CHAPTER 24

EMMA

*I*t's after five o'clock by the time I reach Wonder Time Toys, and Carrie is almost ready to clock out. "Just give me fifteen or twenty minutes to finish the order forms with Phil, and then we'll get out of here, get some sushi, and make big plans."

"I can't eat sushi," I say numbly, shell-shocked by the events of the day. A part of me still can't believe I'm pregnant, even though I'm the proud owner of a black and white printout of the precious dot growing inside of me.

"That's right! Sushi's off-limits for the preggers, isn't it?" She waves a dismissive hand. "Then we'll get Cuban or soul food or something, whatever sounds good to you. Ten minutes and I'm all yours."

"Take your time." I motion toward the far corner of the store. "I'll amuse myself in the baby area."

"The baby area! Oh my God, we're going to have a baby! I'm going to be Aunt Carrie!" She bounces up and down in her motorcycle boots with a *squee* of excitement that makes me laugh.

Who would have guessed my tough nut of a sister was secretly so baby crazy?

I just wish I could be as completely thrilled as she is. I really am *so* happy, but I'm scared, too. There's no way Dylan hasn't found my note by now—he was supposed to get to my place around three-thirty—but so far, my cell has remained silent.

"Okay," Carrie says, backing toward the stock room. "Ten minutes."

I nod in acknowledgement and wander toward the baby section of my sister's groundbreaking toy store. It's a land of bright primary colors and toys made of natural wood and stuffed animals so soft they feel like they were made of angel wings. I find a brown cat with chocolate eyes and bring it to my cheek, chest aching as the whisper-soft fur brushes my skin. This could be my baby's first stuffed animal. In less than a year, this heavenly fluff could be brushing against my child's skin.

I'm still marveling at the surreal, wonderful miraculousness of it all when a winded voice asks, "Is that a stuffed cougar? Does that mean you were thinking about me?"

I turn, eyes flying wide as I spot Dylan a few feet away by a display of Baby's First Building Blocks. "Wh-what are you doing here?" I ask, the thrill that rushes through me at the sight of him tempered by anxiety.

How on earth am I going to keep up this lie with him standing in front of me, staring so deep into my eyes I'm pretty sure he's reading every hidden wish I've ever scrawled across my heart?

"I can't let you do this." He clears his throat and shakes his head. "That didn't come out right. I meant... I hope you'll give me a chance to change your mind. About the sperm bank. I practiced what I was going to say all the way here, but I took one look at you and it all flew out of my head." He runs his hand through his already disheveled hair with a sigh. "It's good to see you, Blondie. I missed you today."

My lips twitch, but I'm too nervous to smile. "I missed you, too. And I'm sorry. I know a note wasn't the best way to handle this, but I—"

"No, it wasn't. But being a vague-ass bastard about something that's so important to you wasn't the best way to handle your question last night, either." He steps closer, his delicious Dylan smell swirling through my head as he takes my hand, pressing it between both of his. "So I'd like to try again, and make it clear to you that if you're having a baby, I want to be the father. And yes, I would rather we wait a few months before we start trying again, just to be one hundred percent sure we're ready, but if you can't wait a few months, then I—"

"It's not that." I pull my hand from his and take a step back, my resolve faltering as the truth shoves at me from the inside, doing its best to break through into the air between us.

But if I tell him the truth, this won't be a choice we're making anymore. It will be a fact he's stuck with, no matter what happens in our future.

"Then what is it?" he asks, uncertainty flickering

across his face. "Have you changed your mind about me? Decided you'd rather have someone with a master's degree and a better sperm pedigree?"

I shake my head. "No, nothing like that."

"I can understand if you did," he says, looking so crestfallen it makes my chest ache. "I was top of my class in high school, but I don't have a college degree or a flashy career. Hell, I've never even lived on my own. I've been under my father's roof since I was a kid."

"Because you've been taking care of him and your nephews and the farm and everything else," I say, refusing to listen to him minimize who he is or all the wonderful things he's accomplished. "You're a savvy, hard-working businessman who not only has a green thumb, but does his own books, to boot. You also happen to be one of the most grown-up, selfless, loving people I've ever met. And that's more impressive to me than a dozen fancy degrees."

Relief and uncertainty mix in his expression. "Then what is it, princess? Tell me what you need from me. I was thinking about this all afternoon and I..." His breath rushes out. "I want to be a part of everything your future holds. I want to see your winery succeed beyond your wildest dreams. I want to watch your garden grow to take up an even more ridiculous amount of your yard. I want to laugh and learn and adventure with you and watch you become the best mom any kid has ever had."

Tears spring into my eyes, blurring his features as my hand comes to cover my mouth.

"I know you will be an incredible mother," he

continues softly. "But no matter what a kick-ass mom she's got, I don't want this kid to ever wonder why her dad isn't around. I want to be right there, every minute. Every second."

I blink, sending twin tear-streams rolling down my face. I'm crying *again*, but I don't think even Carrie would blame me this time. Because that was by far the most romantic, beautiful thing anyone has ever said to me.

"Really?" I ask, with a sniff. "You're serious? And sure? Because once we take this step there's no going back."

"I'm sure," he says, closing the distance between us. "I would hate to lose the chance to be a biological father to your baby because I didn't do a good enough job explaining the way I feel."

I swallow past the lump in my throat and swipe my fingers across my cheeks, regaining control. I don't want to be crying when I tell him the news. I want to have all my wits about me so I can judge his reaction as clearly as possible.

"You've done a beautiful job of telling me the way you feel." I pull in another bracing breath. "But I'm afraid I haven't done the same. I thought I was doing what was best, bending the truth so you would have the freedom to walk away." He frowns, obviously confused, so I hurry on, "But you don't want to walk away."

"I sure as hell don't," he says. "But I don't understand what you're saying."

"I'm saying that I'm not going to the sperm bank. I

don't have to go. Because I'm..." I lift my hands at my sides, fingers spread wide. "...already pregnant."

His eyes go blank for a long moment before he blinks. "I'm sorry, I thought you just said—"

"I went to the doctor this morning for an ultrasound and they confirmed it." I reach into my purse, pulling out the grainy black and white picture and holding it out between us.

Dylan takes the piece of paper carefully, like it's made of baby-delicate stuff, and studies it with a furrowed brow.

"We got pregnant the first night. I didn't realize it because of the spotting, but apparently that's normal and the baby's fine, so..." I trail off, toes squirming anxiously inside my boots. "Please say something. Or at least look at me, so I have some idea what you're thinking."

He looks up, eyes bright. "We're pregnant? We're going to have baby?"

I nod. "Looks like the Hunter baby-making gene didn't skip a generation."

A slow smile spreads across his face in response—a delighted, wonder-filled grin that leaves no doubt he's as excited about this baby as I am. "I can't believe it." He reaches out, hand hovering over my belly where our little dot is working hard at growing into a baby. "God, Emma. I... I don't know what to say."

"But you're happy?" I ask, needing to hear the words, even though the way he pulls me into his arms, hugging me tight, is a pretty solid indicator.

"So happy. And shocked, I'll admit it. But excited,

too." He kisses the top of my head before he pulls back, adding in a whisper, "Also a little turned on. Is that weird? That hearing you're having my baby makes me want to bang you by the diaper display?"

I bite my lip. "If it's weird, I'm weird, too. I want you so much. This time with no lame-ass condom."

"Condoms are lame-ass." He kisses me, his hands threading gently into my hair. "But you are sexy as hell, baby. You're going to be one hot fucking mama."

I smile against his lips. "Let's see if you still think that when I'm eight months along and weigh a gajillion pounds"

"You'll still be a smoking hot fox." His hands drift down to cup my ass, pulling me closer to the erection that proves how sexy he finds my knocked-up self. "I'm still going to want to make you come every chance I get."

"Sexy Farmer, I presume?" My sister's voice is close.

Too close.

Close enough that Dylan and I jump apart with guilty laughs to find Carrie a foot away, watching us make out with narrowed eyes.

"Hey, I'm Dylan," he says, extending a hand. "You must be Carrie."

Carrie takes his hand, shaking it firmly. "I am. Is it also safe to presume that you're crazy about my sister and are going to adore and support her in the coming months and fetch her ice cream and anything else her sweet heart desires?"

"I am and I will. Going to be there every step of the way," he says, the words a promise that sends warmth rushing through me, banishing the last lingering bit of worry.

This is right.

This is the way this was always supposed to happen. I don't know that I've ever believed in destiny before, but I believe in it now, and I know that Dylan and I are written in the stars somewhere over Mercyville, California.

Later that night, after we've gotten a room at The Graduate Hotel near the college in order to spare the rickety old bed in Carrie's guest room, Dylan and I prove how well we fit together all over again. As he guides me down onto him in the moonlight, filling me so perfectly, every shift of our hips, every kiss, every touch is another promise that we're all in, no holding back.

"I love you, princess," he says, holding me close as he softens inside me, neither of us in any rush to pull apart. "I'm so glad I'm here with you. There's nowhere else I'd rather be."

"Me, too," I agree, patting the place above his lovely heart. "I've got everything I need. Right here."

Or so I think, until nine months later, when Mercy Elizabeth Haverford Hunter the first makes her appearance on the scene after ten hours of labor and a ridiculous amount of pushing. But the second she looks up at me with her big blue eyes, all the pain and suffering is forgotten.

The universe shifts, the world is reordered, and she slips right into a space between Dylan and me that I hadn't realized was empty until she came to fill it.

To make us a family.

"Oh, she's an angel." I cradle her close, heart growing a dozen sizes larger as her tiny fingers close around one of mine.

"So beautiful," Dylan says with a sniff. "She looks just like you, baby. She's perfect."

I glance over to see tears in his eyes and laugh even as I bring a hand to his face. "Don't cry. She's here and I'm fine. We made it. It's all over now."

"No, it's just beginning." He leans in, pressing a kiss to the blond fuzz on our daughter's head. "We're here for you, baby girl. Always. Me and your mama. You don't ever have to worry whether someone's got your back."

A lump rises in my throat, but before I can take my turn on the teary-go-round, Dylan kisses me, slow and steady, a kiss that assures me of the same things he just promised our baby. That he's always here for me, that he has my back, and that my heart is by far his most treasured possession.

We kiss until Mercy makes a squawking sound that makes us laugh as we glance down into her little face.

"Guess she's ready to meet the rest of her crew," Dylan says, kissing my cheek. "You ready? Or do you want me to tell the savages prowling outside that we want to spend the first night with her alone?"

"No, show them in," I say, excited for my sister and

the wonderful men who have made me a member of their family to meet our sweet girl. "I'm ready."

And I am.

Ready for this and all the love and magic the future holds.

EPILOGUE ONE

DYLAN

One year later...

The guests are already seated, the string quartet has started to play, and the flower girls are walking down the aisle, but the bride is still nursing the baby in the back garden, and I'm pretty sure I've got baby food on the lapel of my tuxedo.

In other words, it's another day in paradise.

Am I cheesy bastard who loves his life, his soon-to-be wife, and his sweet baby girl?

Why yes. Yes, I am, and I'm not about to apologize for it.

A year ago, if you'd told me the first IPA from my new brewery, Chopper Hops, would be winning double gold at the harvest fair, I might have believed you. That was the big dream, after all. But if you'd told me I'd also be the father of the cutest, sweetest little girl in the world—Little Blondie has the market cornered on both, trust me—and about to marry my best friend, I'd have said you were flat out delusional.

But it's all true.

This is my life, and it is filled with more love and happiness than I realized were possible until this amazing woman came into my world.

"Hey, baby. You ready to go?" I jog into the garden as Emma is retying the bow holding up the top of her dress. A few feet away, Mercy toddles unsteadily across the paving stones on chubby legs, headed for the red and orange flowers she likes to grab and shove in her mouth at every opportunity.

Thank God they're edible.

"Yes, just a sec." Emma stands, smoothing the front of her dress as she turns to me with a smile that takes my breath away. "What do you think?"

"Beautiful," I say, throat going tight. "You're the most beautiful thing I've seen."

Her grin stretches wider as her cheeks flush. "Thank you. You're not too shabby yourself. But I didn't mean that." She smoothes her hand self-consciously over her belly. "I meant, can you tell?"

I narrow my eyes at the ever-so-slight bump beneath her gown. "I can, but it's not going to show in the pictures."

"Are you sure?" Her brow furrows as she hurries toward Mercy, who is already shoving flower number two between her lips and burbling happily to herself. "I just don't want it to be too obvious."

"It won't be," I promise. "But we should probably—"

"Time to bounce, you two." Jacob hurries around the

corner with Blake close behind. "We're on Mercy duty. You two go get married."

"Yeah," Blake says. "The last bridesmaid is on her way down the aisle."

"Don't let Mercy eat any more flowers," I say, reaching for Emma.

"Or dirt," she says, squeezing my palm with one hand while she gathers the skirt of her lace dress with the other.

And then we're off, jogging around the side of the house and down the hill to the patch of grass near the vineyard where our family and friends are seated in rows of white chairs, waiting to celebrate with us. And every one of them—even Rafe, who hates weddings with a rabid passion, and Carrie, who swears marriage is a broken, archaic institution—is smiling ear to ear.

That's what happens when you're in the presence of love like this—love that's right, real, and accompanied by a hundred daily acts of devotion that speak louder than any words ever could.

It lights you up. It spreads. It multiplies.

So really, you can't blame Emma or me for being already knocked up a second time. Love's to blame. And condoms. Or lack thereof.

Turns out Emma and I really don't care for condoms...

Good thing we *really* like babies.

We reach the end of the thick blue runner laid out over the grass and slow to a walk, grinning like crazy people as we walk down the aisle hand-in-hand, giving ourselves to each other for as long as we both shall live.

And I sure hope that's a long, long time, because I'm never going to get tired of making love or laughs or babies with this woman.

She taught me to reach for my dreams, to be thankful for all the gifts in my life, and to love without holding back. She made me treasure my family even more than I did before, and gave me a family of my own, a gift so beautiful I can't believe I thought I was complete without it.

"You are my best friend, my partner, my love, and my life," I say, gazing deep into Emma's eyes as we near the end of our vows. "You are my partner in crime, the keeper of my secrets, and the best mom any kid ever had. You make me excited to wake up every morning, because I get to share another adventure with you, Emma Haverford. I will love you all the days of my life and all the days after."

She sniffs, lips pressing together as she shakes her head slightly from side to side. "I should give up on the whole trying-not-to-cry thing, right?"

Our gathered family and friends laugh, I smile, and then take my turn getting choked up as Emma recites the same vow to me.

By the end, we're both choked up, but that doesn't make our first kiss as husband and wife any less sweet.

Later, as we're dancing under paper lanterns strung through the trees at the vineyard's edge, we make more promises and plans. We float ideas for future adventures, laugh at Mercy's face as she tries her first bite of wedding cake and decides it's even better than flowers, and debate whether or not Finn is an acceptable name for a baby boy who isn't also a fish.

And, of course, we fall deeper in love, the way we have every night since the night Emma made me an offer I couldn't refuse beneath a harvest moon.

EPILOGUE THE SECOND

RAFE

*W*eddings.

Gag me with the sharp end of the bouquet.

No offense to those who enjoy this kind of shit, but I'd rather be dragged naked through the streets behind a speeding Harley.

My brother's wedding is better than most—Dylan and Emma are crazy about each other and can't seem to stop having kids, so it makes sense for them to take the plunge, I guess—but all the sappiness in the air is still making me queasy.

Romancing the shit out of a woman is one thing.

Getting teary-eyed over the wedding vows is another.

As soon as the toasts and the first dance are over, I beat it to the parking lot, knowing I won't be missed. The bride and groom are too busy making goo-goo eyes at each other, and everyone else is too drunk, seeing as the wedding started forty-five minutes late and Emma's tasting room staff was pouring hefty samples while we waited.

I, however, only had one glass. I knew a quick getaway was in my future.

But when I reach my bike, I find my baby—a vintage 1950 Harley Panhead I coaxed back to glory with my own two hands—hemmed in by two Smart cars. "What's Smart about an overpriced novelty baby stroller," I grumble, cursing beneath my breath.

"Not to mention poor handling around corners, a less than stellar safety rating, and the fact that they look really, *really* stupid." The husky voice comes from the shadows beneath a live oak. A second later, the most dangerous blonde at the party steps into the light streaming from the lamps on the porch, looking as drop-dead sexy as ever.

With her shoulder-length bleached blond hair dyed purple at the tips, thick eyeliner that accentuates wild blue-purple eyes, and a body made for the black leather bustier and long, gauzy skirt she's wearing, Carrie Haverford checks all of my boxes.

She's also my new sister-in-law and completely off-limits.

I don't have many rules when it comes to women, but I don't fuck where I eat, and I'll have to face this woman over too many holiday dinner tables to risk a one-night stand.

Or however long we would last.

Judging by the sway of her hips as she slinks over to sit on the hood of the red car in front of my bike, it wouldn't be long. She looks like a man-eater, this one.

Be still my raging hard-on…

God, I love bad girls who know what they want. They're even better than good girls desperate to prove how bad they can be with the right guy.

"Looks like you're stuck, bucko," Carrie says with a sigh. "I feel for you. I'm staying in Emma's new guest cottage, which means I'm trapped in happy-ever-after-land."

I laugh as I slide my hands into the pockets of my tux pants, the better to keep them to myself. "Don't tell me you hate weddings, too?"

"Like carpet burns on my ass," she says, filling my filthy mind with images of things I could do to her curvy body that would cause such a thing. "Marriage is just another sickness inflicted upon society by the development of agriculture. It's about property, not love everlasting." She tosses her head, shifting thick blond and purple locks off her forehead, revealing more of her doll-perfect face. "And people weren't intended to be monogamous. Science proved that years ago."

I arch a brow, intrigued. "Really? How's that?"

"Lots of different sources and studies, but the most compelling to me is the design of your gear shift." She grins as her gaze drops to the front of my pants before sliding slowly back up to meet my eyes.

"Yeah? How so?" I murmur, getting thicker in spite of myself.

A hot body is reasonably easy to resist, but a sexy, shifty little mind like hers does me in every time.

"The male member is designed to suction out other men's sperm before it makes its own special delivery," she says, eyes dancing into mine, issuing a challenge I know I have to refuse. "We were meant to be wild things who don't give a damn about who belongs to who. Doesn't that sound nice?"

"Better than nice. It sounds natural," I grunt. "And sane."

Her eyes narrow as she nods. "Totally. Why can't everyone else see that *they're* the crazy ones? Why must they judge us, Valentine?"

My grin stretches wider. "Everyone calls me Rafe. I told you that last time we met, Carrie."

"As I hope I've made clear, I don't care what everyone else does." She stands, hips swaying temptingly beneath her skirt as she moves closer. "I would rather call you Valentine Huxley Raphael, if that's all right."

I curse. "Who told you?"

"Dylan, when he was drunk at the brewery grand opening." She straightens the flower in my lapel, making me powerfully aware of how close she is and how incredible she smells. Like orange blossoms and spice. "Did you know your second name means 'inhospitable place,' Mr. Hunter?"

"But my first name means strong and healthy." I tip my head down, bringing my face closer to hers. "And my third name means God has healed, so I figure two out of three isn't bad. But there's a more pressing question on my mind right now, Trouble."

Her smile stretches wider, proving she likes it when people call her on her mischief. "Yes? What's that, Valentine?"

"Why have you been looking up the meaning of my many ridiculous names?"

"Why, because I want to do bad things to you in the dark, silly," she says in a husky voice. She presses up on tiptoe until our lips are barely an inch apart. "What about you? You up for a top-secret night? You and me, nothing off-limits, and in the morning, we part ways and never say a word about it to each other or anyone else in this family ever again?"

I should say no.

I really, really should...

But I've never been good at "no" or "should," and she's making a compelling argument.

If we stick to Trouble's terms, what could go wrong?

To be continued in THE TROUBLEMAKER... Keep reading for a sneak peek!

Available now where you like to buy books.

SNEAK PEEK!

Enjoy this extended sneak peek from THE
TROUBLEMAKER, Rafe and Carrie's story!

Rafe

So far, so good...

The eggs and bacon have been dispersed, and we're
passing around the pastry plate, but there's still no sign
of Carrie. If my luck holds, I'll be able to wolf down
breakfast, plead urgent work at the shop as an excuse to
leave early, wish Dylan and Emma a happy start to
many years of wedded bliss, and get out of here before
another encounter with Emma's sister.

We escaped disaster last night, but if I have to spend
much more time in Carrie Haverford's violet-eyed,
plush-lipped, sexy-as-hell presence, I'm going to do
something I'll regret. Like invite her onto the back of
my bike, drive out to my favorite secluded, oceanside

cliff, and fuck her senseless on the blanket I keep in my saddlebag.

I spent half the night dreaming about her curves stretched out on soft gray wool, her legs spread to welcome my mouth between her thighs, her gorgeous body rippling beneath mine as my gear shift and I gave her the ride of her life.

I would *very* much like to make Carrie Haverford come screaming my name—pleasuring a woman who has the experience to appreciate an extraordinary lay is something I find very fucking satisfying. But if I stick my dick in my sister-in-law's sister, I'll be giving drama a handwritten, engraved invitation, and that's just not my style.

"How are your eggs?" Dylan asks, nudging my elbow with his.

"Good," I say around a mouthful of bacon. "Gone."

"I noticed. I haven't seen you eat this fast since you quit wrestling junior year." My brother sighs. "Guess you're aiming to get out of here before the shit hits the fan?"

I glance his way, brows lifting. Concern tickles the hairs at the back of my neck, but I ignore it. There's no way Dylan knows what almost happened with Carrie last night. Whatever he's talking about, it has nothing to do with me.

"You haven't heard?" He shakes his head before continuing in a softer voice, "Carrie's ex leaked nude pictures of her to the press."

My eyes go wide and anger flares hot and sudden in

my chest. "What the fuck? What kind of piece of shit does that?"

"The kind who doctored her PowerPoint presentation so nude photos popped up on the screen while she was giving a talk to some middle school kids last week," Dylan says, frowning as I start to choke on my orange juice. "You didn't know?"

I shake my head with a cough. "No."

"That's why Carrie moved into our guest cottage. She was hoping if she stayed off the grid, the scandal would blow over. But now her ex has taken it to the next level."

I curse softly, the urge rising inside me to find this coward and punch his balls so far into his abdomen he'll still be digging them out next Christmas. But I stopped tackling problems with my fists years ago and Carrie's problems aren't mine to solve.

Still, I can't help wondering... "So what's next? Is she going to take legal action?"

Dylan shrugs as he stabs another bite of scrambled eggs. "I'm not sure. It just happened a couple of hours ago. Emma's going to talk to her after breakfast. I don't know what they'll decide, but if it were up to me, we'd absolutely lawyer up and go after this guy. Embarrassing her is bad enough, but he's deliberately trying to wreck her career while he's at it."

I'm about to agree with him when Emma appears behind Dylan's chair, a sticky-faced, syrup-drenched blond cherub in her arms. "Mercy got ahold of the syrup again," she says breathlessly, as my niece giggles and thrashes her arms and legs, clearly pleased with herself and the mess she's made. "Can you help me get her out of these clothes and into the bath?"

"On it." Dylan tosses his napkin on the table as he stands. "You start the water, I'll get her out of her dress and put it in the sink to soak."

The happy couple hurries into the house while the wedding party continues to feast upon eggs, bacon, pastries, and several pounds of fresh fruit and berries. My dad is holding court at the far end of the table, torturing my nephews and their girlfriends with stories from his glory days, while my oldest brother, Deacon, shovels it in with the single-minded focus of a lifelong military man accustomed to eating far inferior food. Next to Deacon, Emma's mother flirts with Farmer Stroker, even though our eighty-year-old neighbor is ancient enough to be her father. Closer to my end of the table, beside Emma's empty chair, my younger brother Tristan speaks earnestly with the minister who married Emma and Dylan, both of them looking far too somber for people celebrating the union of a couple who are madly in love.

But the minister—Father Pete, a family friend who went to school with Deacon before going to Episcopal seminary—is getting a divorce, and my brother recently broke up with his girlfriend of over a decade. I doubt either of them feel much like celebrating, and though I respect Pete and love my baby brother, I don't want to get sucked into whatever sad-clown fest they're having.

I would prefer not to get sucked into *any* further conversation, as a matter of fact, and with Dylan and

Emma gone and everyone else engaged, I sense the moment to escape is at hand.

After wiping my mouth discreetly, I place my napkin beside my empty plate, take a last drink of fresh OJ, and slide from my chair. I slip around the tall shrubs at the edge of Emma's impressive garden, and a moment later I'm out of sight, following the paving stone trail around to the front of the house, making a mental note to text Dylan and thank him for breakfast when I get home.

He won't mind that I bailed without a formal good-bye. Dylan and I might only be half-brothers, but we've been best friends since we were five years old. He knows ghosting is part of who I am, and not a part I'm ever going to apologize for. Goodbyes aren't my thing, especially big family goodbyes that take half an hour to get everyone out the door.

My bike is parked by the house for an easy getaway, and I'm nearly home free when a flash of light and color on the porch draws my focus.

I glance over, meeting a lavender-blue gaze so sad the emotion reverberates through my chest like a mallet lobbed into a drum. Immediately, I slow, turning to face the woman huddled in the red rocking chair with her knees drawn in to her chest.

Yes, I was hoping to make my escape without seeing Carrie, but I can't leave her like this—braced for the next bomb to hit and clearly on the verge of tears.

"Hey." I prop my hands low on my hips. "Not up for breakfast?"

She shakes her head. "I was headed that way, but then my agent's assistant texted to tell me my speaking gigs for the rest of the summer have been cancelled, so…"

I sigh. "I heard about what happened. What your ex did. I'm sorry."

Carrie winces as her focus drops to the dusty ground at my feet. "Thanks. So… I guess everyone has seen them, then? The pictures?"

"I haven't. And I won't go looking," I assure her. "No one here will."

"Thanks." Her lips twist. "But I'm sure my mom is going to hunt them down. And when she sees them, I'm going to get a lecture about the importance of professional lighting, especially when taking one's clothes off, and why I should stop trusting people because I'm a shit judge of character."

Hmmm… Mom issues. Not surprising from what I've seen of her mother so far, but definitely not something I want to get into. I don't do issues. I offloaded mine in junior high, perfected not giving a shit in high school, and embraced the Zen lifestyle fully as an adult. Not sweating life's bullshit is something I take pride in, and a trait I seek out in other people.

If you're looking for a shoulder to cry on, I'm not your man, not by a long shot.

I'm about to say something kind but vague—*sorry again, hope things get better*, or some such—when Carrie stands, stretching her arms high over her head, causing her breasts to strain the front of her pale purple tank top.

My mouth goes dry and my pulse picks up, throbbing in my throat. God, she's beautiful. Perfectly made from the tip of her button nose to the tips of all the other parts that I shouldn't be *thinking* about, let alone openly drooling over.

Exerting more willpower than I would like, I wrench my gaze from her chest as her arms fall to her sides.

"Forget it," she says. "I don't want to talk about this shit, and I'm sure you don't, either. And I can handle breakfast. I have to handle it." She sighs as she jabs a thumb toward the driveway. "When I moved my car last night, I guess I didn't shut the door all the way after. Stupid battery is dead. Until I get a jump, I'm trapped."

Trapped. It's one of my least favorite things in the world. And judging from her tone, I'm guessing it's not high on her list, either.

"But you'd rather run?' I ask. "If you had the chance?"

She huffs a soft, "Oh yeah. Much rather."

I let out a measured breath, weighing my options. The smart thing would be to tell her goodbye and good luck, jump on my Harley, and get the hell out of here before I do something I'll regret. The kinder choice would be to give her a jump and send her on her way alone, ensuring she has the juice to run as far and as fast as she needs to in order to escape the misery weighing her down.

But when her full lips tremble and her violet eyes begin to shine, I find myself jerking my head toward my bike. "Come on. Let's go for a ride."

She blinks, shoulders rolling away from her ears as she stands up straighter. "Really?"

"Really. I've got an extra helmet and nowhere special to be."

With a soft yip of excitement, she jumps over the porch railing to land lightly on the ground in front of me. A moment later, her arms are around my neck, her curves pressing against my chest as she locks me into a surprisingly powerful hug. "Thank you, Rafe. Really. I appreciate it. I could use a friend this morning."

"No problem." I return the embrace with one arm, trying not to notice how perfectly she fits against me or how amazing she smells. She said it herself—she needs a friend, which is perfect because that's all she and I are ever going to be.

Carrie and I are friends.

Friends, I repeat silently as she settles onto the bike behind me, her thighs sliding against mine, her arms locking around my waist, and her breasts soft and tempting against my back.

Friends don't give friends raging erections, asshole.

The inner voice is right, of course. But my dick doesn't give two shits about right or wrong, and by the time we pull out onto the highway, I'm as hard as a steel pike and not sure who will win out in a battle of wills— the logical inner voice or the hunger curling low and tight inside me, whispering that sometimes rules are meant to be broken.

Available now where you like to buy books!

TELL LILI YOUR FAVORITE PART!

I love reading your thoughts about the books and your review matters. Reviews help readers find new-to-them authors to enjoy. So if you could take a moment to leave a review letting me know your favorite part of the story —nothing fancy required, even a sentence or two would be wonderful—I would be deeply grateful.

Thank you and happy reading!

ABOUT THE AUTHOR

Author of over forty novels, *USA Today* Bestseller **Lili Valente** writes everything from swoony small town romance to laugh-out-loud romantic comedies. A die-hard romantic, she can't resist a story where love wins big. When she's not writing, Lili enjoys adventuring with her two sons and puppy Pippa Jane.

Find Lili at...
www.lilivalente.com

Banging The Enemy

The Rock Star's Baby Bargain

Hometown Heat Series

All Fired Up

Catching Fire

Playing with Fire

A Little Less Conversation

The Bliss River Small Town Series

Falling for the Fling

Falling for the Ex

Falling for the Bad Boy

The Hunter Brothers

The Baby Maker

The Troublemaker

The Heartbreaker

The Panty Melter

Big O Dating Specialists
Romantic Comedies

Hot Revenge for Hire

Hot Knight for Hire

Hot Mess for Hire

Hot Ghosthunter for Hire

The Lonesome Point Series

(Sexy Cowboys)

Leather and Lace

Saddles and Sin

Diamonds and Dust

12 Dates of Christmas

Glitter and Grit

Sunny with a Chance of True Love

Chaps and Chance

Ropes and Revenge

8 Second Angel

The Good Love Series

(co-written with Lauren Blakely)

The V Card

Good with His Hands

Good to be Bad

The Happy Cat Series

(co-written with Pippa Grant)

Hosed

Hammered

Hitched

Humbugged

Made in the USA
Columbia, SC
12 August 2022